A wild r...

D1276587

Lucas zoomed over the .... rider. Clinging to Lucas's neck, Vanessa screamed as the horse broke into a full gallop and headed down the drive, straight toward the main road.

"Get in my car!" yelled Ms. P. Sophie and Cara dashed to the station wagon and jumped in.

Ms. P. drove full speed down the drive. They rounded a bend just in time to see Lucas jump a hedge, unseating Vanessa. She flipped over his head and fell hard on her shoulders. Lucas slowed down, and finally stopped.

"Let me get him," Cara begged.

Ms. P. stopped the car by Vanessa, who lay white and unconscious in the mud. Cara gently approached Lucas.

"Lucas, it's me," she whispered.

Hearing her voice seemed to calm him. She gathered up his tangled reins and with infinite tenderness ran her hands along his neck.

"Shh, shh, it's all right," she murmured. She talked to him and stroked him until he seemed completely calmed down, then walked him back to the stable. There she untacked him and washed his wounds.

"I'll look after you for a while," she promised.

She had never felt so useless. Lucas, the love of her life, was at great risk, and all she could do was stand by and watch. Surely somebody could stop this cruelty!

Collect all the books in Joanna Campbell's
THOROUGHBRED series

And look for

*coming soon

ATTENTION: ORGANIZATIONS AND CORPORATIONS

Most HarperPaperbacks are available at special quantity
discounts for bulk purchases for sales promotions, premiums,
or fund-raising. For information, please call or write:
Special Markets Department, HarperCollins Publishers,
10 East 53rd Street, New York, N.Y. 10022
Telephone: (212) 207-7528. Fax: (212) 207-7222.

THE MOST BEAUTIFUL HORSE IN THE WORLD

DIANE REDMOND

HarperPaperbacks

A Division of HarperCollins*Publishers*

For my daughter, Tamsin,
and Lucas, himself!

If you purchased this book without a cover, you should be
aware that this book is stolen property. It was reported as
"unsold and destroyed" to the publisher and neither the
author nor the publisher has received any payment for this
"stripped book."

This is a work of fiction. The characters, incidents, and
dialogues are products of the author's imagination and are not
to be construed as real. Any resemblance to actual events or
persons, living or dead, is entirely coincidental.

HarperPaperbacks   *A Division of* HarperCollins*Publishers*
               10 East 53rd Street, New York, N.Y. 10022

Copyright © 1994 by Diane Redmond and
Daniel Weiss Associates, Inc.

Cover art copyright © 1994 Daniel Weiss Associates, Inc.

All rights reserved. No part of this book may be used or
reproduced in any manner whatsoever without written
permission of the publisher, except in the case of brief
quotations embodied in critical articles and reviews. For
information address Daniel Weiss Associates, Inc., 33 West
17th Street, New York, New York 10011.

Produced by Daniel Weiss Associates, Inc., 33 West 17th
Street, New York, New York 10011.

First printing: February, 1994

Printed in the United States of America

HarperPaperbacks and colophon are trademarks of
HarperCollins*Publishers*

10 9 8 7 6 5 4 3 2 1

1

CARA TIGHTENED HER GRIP ON THE DOUBLE-REINED BRIDLE and pulled Fancy down into a smooth canter, glancing anxiously at the rooftops of Hunters' Riding School. Ms. P., the owner and a formidable ex-three-day eventer, would be checking her watch, expecting them back precisely at six.

"Why does my one precious hour of riding a week flash by?" she asked her best friend, Tansy Miller. From underneath her hard hat Tansy's long blond hair blew across her face, but Cara could still see her grin.

"Because it's free!" Tansy answered. "Come on, race you back!" Digging her heels into Shadow's dark flanks, Tansy shot ahead of Cara. Cara quickly urged Fancy into a gallop, overtaking Tansy with ease.

"Hey! No fair!" Tansy shouted. "Fancy's younger than Shadow."

"And in better shape!" Cara yelled over her shoulder.

The girls had ridden together since first grade, when they'd both fallen in love with horses and started riding lessons at Ms. P.'s school. Every Saturday they took an hour lesson at the school, working their way up from the smallest ponies to the largest, and now to horses. But an hour a week just wasn't enough.

"Please, Mom, let me have another hour," Cara had begged for years.

"Sweetheart, we can't do it." Mrs. Zol's answer was always the same. "An hour a week is absolutely all we can afford."

Like most families in Shannon, Virginia, Cara's family was on a tight budget. Mrs. Zol worked as a secretary for Lionel Roberts, a local big-time building contractor and self-made millionaire, and Mr. Zol was a mechanic. Although through hard work the Zols had always been able to provide Cara and her seven-year-old brother, Mike, with essentials, buying a horse was out of the question.

At last Cara had partly resigned herself to the situation. A single hour of riding a week was better than nothing, and that single hour was the highlight of her week. The weekdays were just a countdown to Saturday, when Cara was up at dawn, pacing the house and trying to hurry her mother to the stables.

"Give me a break!" Mrs. Zol laughed as Cara rushed her through breakfast. "It's only eight thirty, and your lesson doesn't start till ten!"

"But I want to *be there*!" Cara said. She loved being around the stables almost as much as riding. The horses and ponies would look expectantly out over their stall doors when they heard her step, waiting for the carrots she gave them when Ms. P. wasn't around. The stables smelled of warm hay and sawdust, and she could hear the horses and ponies stamping and crunching their feed the minute she walked through the doorway. It was always difficult to leave, knowing that a whole week stood between her and the next glorious visit.

But now that she and Tansy were thirteen, Ms. P. permitted them to work around the stables: cleaning tack, grooming the horses, and mucking out stalls. In exchange, they got an extra hour of riding each week free.

"That makes *two* lessons a week," Cara told her parents, her dark blue eyes wide and glowing. "And I only have to pay for one."

Cara had always been a talented rider and quick to learn. Her love of horses and natural abilities, combined with an unusual graceful strength, made her stand out from the other riders in her class. As a result Ms. P. seemed to work her twice as hard as anyone else.

"Sit deeper in the saddle, Cara!" she snapped. "Now you're slouching. Keep those reins down. Why are you flapping your elbows? You're a show jumper—not a goose!"

Sometimes Cara finished her lesson exhausted, her body aching from the workout.

"But she likes you," Tansy insisted one day, joining Cara on a bench outside Fancy's stall.

Cara pulled off one of her high black riding boots and grimaced, rubbing cramped thigh muscles.

"If she likes me any more, she's going to kill me," she said with a giggle. "But I know I should thank her anyway for helping me perfect my position." Cara got up with difficulty and hobbled across the yard. Her legs felt curved like bananas.

"I don't really like her," said Tansy, following Cara. "She scares me."

"She's a perfectionist; I guess she has to be hard," Cara said, trying to pull her shoulder-length black hair into a less disorganized ponytail. Then she frowned.

Eleanor Pryzelomski—always formally addressed by her riders as Ms. P.—coached her riders to the highest standards. They regularly worked the local junior circuit, winning many ribbons and prizes, although Ms. P. seldom lavished praise on anyone. Cara had long secretly suspected that she was Ms. P.'s star pupil, but it was going to be hard to advance much more, especially in jumping, without a horse of her own.

Finally Ms. P. admitted as much one warm spring day, after Cara had turned in a flawless performance in a show-jumping class held at the stables. "I'd like to see you in my office," she said, and from her tone Cara couldn't tell if she was in for a lecture or praise.

Cara sat on a folding chair in the dusty office. Around the walls were photographs of a young Ms. P. during her competition days, perfectly turned out for a dressage class or sailing over a triple gate in a

4

show-jumping final. Cara remembered that as little girls she and Tansy had loved this office. They had always looked for excuses to sneak in and walk around the walls, admiring the photographs and tarnished silver trophies.

A few moments later Ms. P. strode in and perched on the edge of her desk. She said abruptly, "You have a genuine talent for riding."

Cara reddened with surprise and pleasure.

"You have the potential to be a gifted show jumper, but not without a horse of your own."

Cara blushed more deeply, for a different reason. "There's nothing—my parents—"

"I didn't mean to bring up what's old hat. What I want to tell you is this. I'm prepared to lend you a mount and coach you, within reason, but I can't do more than that, even though you show great promise."

Cara stared at Ms. P. Her instructor had never openly praised her before.

"Thank you," she mumbled, overwhelmed by the kind words and Ms. P.'s generosity.

"It's the least I can do," Ms. P. answered, cracking her riding crop against her boot. "You would go further and faster with a horse of your own, but there we are."

Driving home with her mother, Cara tried to think what else she could try on her parents to get them to buy her a horse. Over the years she had cried, begged, pleaded, sulked, and shouted, but nothing had changed the fact that her parents couldn't afford a horse for her.

Several weeks later Cara walked into the house after a long, successful day at the riding school and called, "Hi, everybody! I'm home."

"We're in here," answered her mother from the kitchen.

Cara walked into the kitchen. Her mother, father, and Mike sat around the table. The minute she saw their excited faces, she knew something momentous had happened.

"What is it?" Cara asked nervously, pushing her hair out of her face. Were they moving? Had her mother or father gotten a new job? Maybe they had won the lottery.

"Sweetheart, sit down," Mr. Zol said. "We've got something to tell you."

Cara dropped her riding coat and hat and grabbed the nearest chair. She looked quickly at all three of them in turn.

"Well, tell me!" she cried.

Mike looked at their mother, who turned to Mr. Zol, who smiled back at Mrs. Zol.

"You tell her," Mr. Zol said to his wife, tipping back in his chair. "You masterminded this."

Mrs. Zol smiled secretively. "I'd be happy to. Cara, do you remember my boss's daughter, Stephanie Roberts?"

That spoiled monster, Cara thought. She had never met Stephanie, but Mrs. Zol had told Cara all about her. Cara hadn't the least desire to be acquainted with the girl who had everything: fantastic clothes, a huge house, and a magnificent, costly show jumper.

Cara sighed unhappily. Surely the big news wasn't yet another success story about the great Stephanie Roberts?

"She's going off to Santa Barbara in California to study law," Mrs. Zol continued.

Cara nodded. She knew that too, from the almost nightly reports her mother gave on the Roberts family over dinner. Who cared about Santa Barbara?

"So?" she asked impatiently.

Mrs. Zol smiled, unable to hold back her secret a moment longer. "I asked if you can look after her horse while she's away!"

"Lucas?" Cara gasped. This couldn't be true.

Mrs. Zol nodded. "Lucas," she said firmly.

Lucas, Stephanie Roberts's chestnut gelding, was a family legend. Cara had heard every detail of his dynamic show-jumping career from her mother over many family dinners. In fact, Cara had sometimes stopped listening because the stories made her sick with envy.

"But Mom, Stephanie doesn't even know me," said Cara.

"She does now," Mr. Zol said, smiling. "Your mom's been working on this for a long time."

"After Ms. P. phoned me a few weeks ago—" Mrs. Zol began.

"Ms. P. phoned *you*?" Cara interrupted. "Why?"

"To tell me what a gifted horsewoman you are and how much you need a horse of your own," Mrs. Zol said.

"She told me that too," Cara admitted.

"But you kept it a secret?" Mr. Zol asked.

"It didn't seem like a good idea to keep nagging you," she said pointedly.

"We appreciate that, honey," Mr. Zol replied with a warm smile. "But after that telephone conversation with Ms. P., we decided we were going to move heaven and earth to get you a horse." Mr. Zol ruffled his daughter's dark hair affectionately.

"Wow!" Cara gasped.

"So Mom worked on Mr. Roberts," Mike said excitedly.

"Not at first, Mike," Mrs. Zol corrected him. "When I heard that Stephanie would be leaving this summer but didn't plan to sell Lucas, I talked to Joseph, Lucas's groom."

Cara's heart pounded. "I think I've died and gone to heaven," she whispered.

"That's why we didn't dare tell you until we were sure Lucas was really going to be yours," said Mr. Zol. "We didn't want you to be disappointed."

"I knew everything!" Mike shouted, jumping out of his chair with excitement. "But I kept quiet," he added importantly. Cara smiled at her little brother, who looked like he might pop with happiness.

"You did just fine, Mike," she said, tears suddenly coming to her eyes.

"After I talked to the groom, I approached Mr. Roberts about the horse," Mrs. Zol continued. "He and Stephanie want to meet you on Tuesday."

"*Meet me!*" Cara leaped up from the table. "Oh, Mom! You couldn't be more wonderful!" She ran to her mother and hugged her hard.

"Your mom's a genius," Mr. Zol agreed comfortably.

Cara hugged her dad and Mike too. "Thanks for what you guys did," she whispered.

Mrs. Zol patted her daughter's arm. "Sit down a minute," she said gently. "Don't forget, we've got to get through an interview on Tuesday before we can really celebrate."

Cara gulped. The word *interview* brought her abruptly back to reality.

"Why don't you go over to the Robertses' on Monday after school and introduce yourself to Lucas while no one is around?" Mrs. Zol suggested. "Mr. Roberts will be out of town for the day, and Stephanie's got shopping to do. That will give you some time on your own with him."

Cara nodded, her face aglow. "I'll take the bus over from school," she said. Her pulse quickened. In just a day and a half she'd meet the legendary show jumper Lucas, after years of only hearing about him.

2

TANSY STOOD OPENMOUTHED IN THE HALLWAY AT SCHOOL as Cara poured out her amazing story on Monday morning.

"I don't believe it!" Tansy gasped. "Nobody could be *that* lucky!"

"Yeah, I need somebody to pinch me and tell me I'm not dreaming," Cara said, grinning.

Her classes went by in a blur. Cara even spent math class, which she usually liked, staring out the window at the clouds, wondering about the chances of rain by three o'clock.

The second the last-period bell rang, Cara grabbed her books and flew through the halls to the bus.

"Call me!" Tansy yelled after her. Cara waved as she raced around a corner.

Cara was so excited, she got off at the wrong bus stop and had to take the back road into the Robertses' farm, then cut through the woods. It was a perfect

June day, filled with the joyous chirping of birds in the old beech woods and the delicate scent of wildflowers along the road. In the distance Cara could see an elegant colonial house, with white clapboard gables soaring from every corner. Pink Virginia roses wound their way along the windows almost up to the rooftop. All around the house emerald lawns rolled away into deep woodland.

Breathless with excitement, Cara broke out of the woods, then stopped dead at the edge of a white-fenced paddock. Slowly she leaned on the fence, staring at the horse grazing at the far end of the field. The sun slanted through the trees on his gleaming chestnut coat, turning his silky mane and tail to flames.

"Lucas," Cara whispered. She knew he couldn't have heard her, but he lifted his head and began walking toward her. The horse's beauty, a perfect combination of the finest Arab breeding with the strength of his Irish draft horse line, took her breath away. Cara vaulted over the fence. With a gentle whinny Lucas trotted toward her. He stopped when she did to look her over curiously. Then, shaking his long mane, he took the last few steps and rested his head on top of her shoulder.

"Hello, Lucas," she murmured, running her hand over his velvet nose. "Did anybody ever tell you you're the most beautiful horse in the world?"

"Just what do you think you're doing?" a voice bellowed across the field. "This is private land!"

Shocked out of her dream, Cara jumped, and Lucas shied away. She turned and saw a small, wiry man with spiky gray hair striding angrily across the field toward her.

"I'm sorry," she said. "My mother's Mrs. Zol—she works here. She told me to come by this afternoon."

The man stopped short and smiled suddenly, showing a mouthful of white but very uneven teeth.

"Hey, *I'm* sorry," he said. "You must be Cara." He held out his hand to shake hers. "I'm Joseph, the groom. I was kind of expecting you to come through the front gate," he added with a smile.

"I meant to," Cara admitted, "but I was so excited I got off the bus at the wrong stop." Her eyes were drawn back across the field to Lucas, who was quietly grazing once more. "He's absolutely gorgeous," she said softly.

Joseph nodded and smiled proudly. "He sure is," he agreed. "We all love Lucas around here." He pulled a carrot out of his pocket, and Lucas pricked his ears. "Here, boy! Come and get it," he called. Lucas walked toward Joseph, apparently in no hurry, and gently pushed the groom's shoulder. "All right, here you go, then," said Joseph. The carrot disappeared in seconds, and Lucas's dark eyes searched for more. "I swear if this horse had money, he'd walk down to the store and buy a bag himself," Joseph said with a laugh.

When Lucas realized the treats were gone, he sauntered back to his grazing, and Joseph showed Cara around the stables. The stable yard was immaculate, with hardly a wisp of straw out of place. Even the manure pile was a perfect pyramid shape.

"Wow," said Cara. "Did you do all this yourself?"

"That's what I'm paid for," Joseph said, sounding pleased.

Cara could have spent the whole afternoon in the tack room, admiring the thick, expensive leather of the well-polished English saddles and bridles and the many types of bits. She stopped in front of one wall, covered with pictures of Lucas standing in triumph while he was awarded ribbons and trophies at various shows. "He's magnificent," she breathed.

"He's some horse," Joseph agreed.

Cara eventually tore herself away from the stables and wandered over to her mother's office, tucked between the house and the stable block. She found her typing up a pile of letters.

"Hi, Mom," she called. "I just met Joseph."

"He's nice," Mrs. Zol replied, firmly keeping her eyes on the computer monitor in front of her.

"Yeah," Cara agreed. She gazed lovingly out the window at Lucas, still grazing contentedly in the paddock. "Mom, what if the Robertses reject me as Lucas's rider?"

"They won't!" Mrs. Zol answered briskly.

"You're just saying that," Cara fretted.

"No, I'm saying it because it's the truth and because Ms. P. told me so," Mrs. Zol replied. "Now, stop worrying. You'll make yourself sick."

By Tuesday afternoon Cara *had* made herself almost physically sick with anxiety. What if she blew this interview? Every time she thought of Lucas's

13

dark, trusting eyes and warm, soft muzzle, she ached with love. Although she had seen him less than twenty-four hours ago, it seemed forever. He galloped through her dreams, and she thought about him every minute she was awake.

During the drive to the Robertses' house, Cara and her mother hardly exchanged a word. Cara tried to think of answers to all the questions Stephanie and Mr. Roberts might throw at her. As they drove up to the house, she yearned to fling open the car door and rush across the paddock to hug Lucas.

Mrs. Zol stopped the car and smiled at Cara. "Ready?" she said softly.

Cara nodded. "Thanks, Mom," she whispered. "No matter what happens."

Cara had never before been inside the Robertses' house, and after the cozy simplicity of her mother's office, she was almost overwhelmed by the elegance and beauty of "The Gables." Twinkling chandeliers lit large, comfortable rooms filled with inviting, deep velvet sofas and armchairs. On all the walls were old oil paintings, framed in silver or gold.

Stephanie came quickly into the room. She wore expensive riding jeans and a University of California T-shirt. "Hey, Cara," she said warmly. "It's great you came over. Would you like to see some of my Lucas photograph albums while Dad dishes up the cake?"

"You bet," said Cara, smiling back. She felt less nervous immediately.

Mr. Roberts chatted with Mrs. Zol while he served

14

up coffee and the best thick fudge chocolate cake Cara had ever tasted.

"Your mother suggested I phone Ms. P.," he said. "She thinks you have great potential as a show jumper."

Cara smiled. "I'm glad."

"We are too." Mr. Roberts refilled his coffee cup. "Stephanie's done a lot of work with Lucas, as you can see from all the photographs." He smiled fondly at the pile of albums on the coffee table. Mr. Roberts had been widowed when Stephanie was only a baby, and everybody knew he adored his only child.

"Before my dad falls hopelessly into the doting father routine, let me say a few things." Stephanie looked at her father. "Okay?"

"You're the expert, honey—I just pay the bills," he said, laughing.

"Lucas is a first-class horse. He can go right to the top," Stephanie said, running a hand through her blond-highlighted hair. Cara nodded. She didn't need convincing about Lucas's abilities.

"I'd planned to enter him in the big Culpeper show this spring," Stephanie continued. "But I had exams, and now I'm going on vacation with some friends from school. Then I start at the university in September." She frowned. "So I've wrecked Lucas's chances at Culpeper, and he's hardly been worked at all for a long time. But maybe you can make up for it this summer and enter him in some shows in the fall. It would be a lot of work, though. Will you have time?"

15

"Absolutely," said Cara. She thought, *Forget about school—just let me ride!*

Mrs. Zol raised an eyebrow, as if she had read Cara's mind.

"We had a few arguments ourselves about the relative importance of school and horses," Mr. Roberts said to Stephanie.

"And now look at me," Stephanie said sadly. "Off to college in Santa Barbara, leaving my poor horse behind."

"Tell us about your competition work," Mr. Roberts said to Cara.

Cara swallowed hard. The delicious cake suddenly sank like a brick in her churning stomach.

"I've been in some shows," she said, meeting Stephanie's eyes. "In three—that's all."

"Cara did well in every one," Mrs. Zol said quickly. "Ms. P. would be the first to agree."

"Well, I've evented hundreds of times, and more often than not come home with zilch," Stephanie said, laughing. "It's not the number of entries that counts."

Cara looked at her gratefully, wondering how she could ever have thought for an instant Stephanie was a spoiled monster.

"Winning's hard," Stephanie went on. She picked up one of the photograph albums and riffled its pages. "Behind all of these winning photos is a real story." Tears filled her eyes as she gazed at a photograph of Lucas flying over a triple gate. "It takes time and talent to win, and luck, and *money*! Your cue,

16

Dad, before I get too emotional." She quickly wiped her eyes. "It'll be hard leaving him," she admitted.

"I'll take care of the costs—you just enjoy Lucas," Mr. Roberts said to Cara. "Give him the kind of challenge he needs, come home with a few rosettes, and we'll all be happy."

Cara stared at him, incredulous. They were going to let her ride Lucas! "Oh, I will!" she promised.

"Then we have a deal." Mr. Roberts beamed and stood up to shake her hand.

Cara stared at him, radiant with happiness. "Is that it?" she asked.

"One more thing," Stephanie added suddenly. "Love him."

"Love him?" Cara laughed and threw her arms around Stephanie. "I *adore* him!"

3

"THAT HORSE HAS YOU RIGHT WHERE HE WANTS YOU," Joseph remarked as he watched Cara hold out first her right fist, then her left in front of Lucas's nose.

Ignoring Joseph's teasing, Cara said, "Guess which hand has the carrot?" Lucas, his dark eyes bright with excitement, sniffed and nuzzled each hand. Cara laughed at his eagerness.

"Choose!" she said. To her delight, Lucas nudged the hand with the carrot and pushed open her fingertips.

"Clever boy." Cara rubbed the horse's sleek neck. "I'm impressed. See, Joseph, he knows his left from his right."

Joseph burst out laughing. "He knows carrots, all right. He could track them down anywhere."

"I think he's a genius," Cara insisted. "The smartest horse in Virginia!"

"He may be smart, but he still needs a good

18

grooming," Joseph reminded her. "Unless you want the farrier to see him covered with mud."

Cara clipped a lead shank to Lucas's halter, led him out of the yard into the stable, and crosstied him in the aisle. She grabbed a dandy brush from his tack box and began cleaning his dirty coat.

"You've got to stop rolling," she told him as she brushed the soft curve of his muddy flanks. "Look at this coat. And what about all the work you've made for me?"

Lucas nudged her and shook his elegant head, as if to say, Aren't I worth every second?

Cara smiled to herself as she brushed him until his golden coat gleamed like fire in the sun. The last few weeks had been wild—she'd spent every possible hour with Lucas, getting to know him, while juggling school at the same time. But with school out and the summer before her, Cara felt like she was in paradise. Just being with Lucas was a joy. Grooming him, cleaning out his stall and his hooves, preparing his feed, and polishing his tack were all part of loving and looking after him. Doing all these jobs had brought them close very quickly. And Lucas's easy, sunny disposition made getting to know him that much easier.

Joseph supervised most of the chores to start with, but soon turned them over to Cara.

"You'll get fed up with all the hard work before long," he said as she shoveled manure out of Lucas's stall into a wheelbarrow.

"Nope," Cara replied firmly. "I've waited all my

life for a dream horse like Lucas. You won't catch me complaining." Whistling, she finished loading up the wheelbarrow and trundled it across the yard to the manure pile. Her years of riding, she knew, had made her stronger than she looked.

"She's a good kid," Joseph told Mrs. Zol one afternoon when she arrived to take Cara home. "Nothing fazes her."

As July turned into August, Joseph increased Cara's workload. He took her along in the summer's heat to different feed stores, where they bought the best cutting of hay for winter feed and straw for bedding. They repaired a sagging stable door, nailed loose boards on the paddock fences, moved the manure pile farther from the stables, and mowed the long grass in one of the paddocks. Out in the sun for twelve hours a day, Cara turned a deep tan, and freckles sprinkled her nose. She visited the vet with Stephanie and went through Lucas's medical files, checking when he had gotten his last shots and worming.

"I have no idea what I'd do without you," Stephanie said one morning as she watched Cara carefully measure Lucas's grain.

Cara picked up the feed bucket and looked at her, surprised. "I don't know what *I'd* do without *you*," she said.

"We're lucky to have each other," Stephanie answered firmly.

Cara had much to do and much to learn. Fortunately she had Joseph to advise and comment.

"We don't want to upset that old horse, do we?" he said to Cara. "With you around all the time, he'll be well used to you by September when Stephanie goes away."

In the beginning, Cara didn't know if she should ride Lucas or wait for Stephanie to come by the stables and ride him. Stephanie soon straightened out the difficulty.

"Look, it's going to be a long summer if you hang around waiting for me to show up," she said. "I'm spending a lot of time with my friends from school because I won't see much of them after I leave for California. Plus I've got some course reading to do before then. So just start riding Lucas whenever you want."

"Great!" Cara said happily. She immediately planned a long ride for the next day.

Soon her favorite ride was up Roly's Hill, a high ridge with magnificent views over the countryside. The springy turf was beautifully smooth and fell effortlessly away under Lucas's galloping hooves. Going up the hill, Lucas would accelerate underneath her like a powerful race car. Whether she rode in the wind, rain, sun, or mist, the jolt of speed and hammering of Lucas's hooves always snatched her breath away and made her giddy with excitement. Cara would hold him to a tight canter until the hill flattened at the top, then relax her grip. As they reached the edge of the ridge and the view spread out before them like a patchwork quilt, Lucas would check his speed, as if he too wanted to enjoy the scenery.

21

Sometimes Cara pulled him to a stop so that she could think quietly for a few minutes, looking at the swell of the land and breathing in the sweet, fresh air.

Cara loved those moments up on the hill, with the wind in her face and the clouds racing overhead. Sharing such times with Lucas bound them even closer together.

Summer faded into early autumn. A soft gold lingered in the air, forming halos around the trees and turning the cobwebs that hung in their branches a magical gray. Early one misty September morning Stephanie and her father loaded Stephanie's trunks into the waiting car. Joseph, Cara, and Mrs. Zol watched them prepare to go. When the moment of departure came, Stephanie's forced cheerfulness cracked.

"Oh, Cara!" she said, her eyes brimming with tears. "Take good, good care of him."

"I will—I promise," Cara answered, her eyes filling too.

With a final wave, Stephanie jumped into the car and was gone. Cara waited until the car had turned at the end of the long drive. Then she hurried off to cuddle Lucas, suddenly feeling overwhelmed by her responsibilities.

"You'll do fine," Joseph reassured her later that day. Cara sat in the tack room, polishing Lucas's bit until it shone like silver. "Lucas loves you to pieces." He grinned. "Of course I have no idea why—it can't have anything to do with the way you spoil him rotten."

Cara smiled. She was getting used to Joseph's teasing. "He knows we're going places together."

Joseph tossed a clean rag at her. "Not until you oil that saddle."

School didn't begin just for Stephanie, far away in California. Cara started eighth grade, and she found it much more demanding than seventh. At the end of the first week, Cara poured out all her fears to Tansy in the school cafeteria.

"Sometimes I feel totally scared," she confessed.

"Of Lucas?" Tansy cried. "Come on!"

"No, not him; he's wonderful." Cara sighed dreamily at the mere thought of Lucas. "It's just—trying to keep *everybody* happy."

"Who's everybody?" Tansy asked.

"Mom, Dad, Mr. Roberts, Joseph, Lucas—and me!" Cara added with a grin. "I have to try to keep all of those people happy every single day."

Cara's days were definitely action-packed. To make time after school to ride Lucas, she was up at six, studying before breakfast. At lunch hour she usually tried to catch up with her homework. After school she didn't hang out with her friends anymore, because she had to dash for the bus and take the half-hour ride to the stables. Lucas, though, always gave her a rapturous reception, trotting across the field and whickering for carrots and cuddles. Then she took him inside and groomed him, telling him all about her day as she ran the dandy brush over him. When his coat gleamed a perfect gold, she tacked him up and rode him along the bridle paths through the woods, now strewn with red and yellow autumn leaves. By six she was back in the stable, mixing Lucas's feed, then she had to race to catch the last bus of the day home. After supper she worked some more on her homework, but often she could hardly keep her eyes from closing. Her mother usually found her fast asleep with a book in her hand, the bedside light still on.

But it was worth it. All of it was worth it—just to be with Lucas. Just the sight of him, grazing in the field, swept all her worry and exhaustion away.

"Hi, buddy!" she would call, and with a soft whinny he would trot toward her, his head high and his eyes fixed on her. "Is it me you want or the carrots?" she sometimes asked. Lucas would nudge her pockets and sniff her hands until he found his treats. Then, like a dog, he would follow her into the yard. She crosstied him in the stable and groomed him thoroughly, brushing his coat until it glowed in the autumn sunshine. He enjoyed her attention, standing still with his eyes half closed as she combed his mane and long tail, picked his hooves, and wiped his eyes and nose clean. Sometimes he'd nudge her off balance as she stooped to pick out his hooves, or push her when she stopped brushing his neck, as if to encourage her to keep going. She got to know his preferences. For example, he liked to be groomed outside the stable so that he could watch the goings-on in the yard.

"He doesn't miss a thing," Joseph remarked one

afternoon as Cara tacked up and he swept the yard clean.

"He enjoys checking *you* out," Cara teased, and added proudly, "Doesn't he look handsome today?'

"Just about perfect," Joseph replied. "Some hoof oil would give his feet a nice shine."

Even though by now Cara had learned her way around the stables, she was still glad to have Joseph's advice and support. He always knew exactly what needed to be done for Lucas: when to bring him in or change his diet, when to call the vet or schedule the farrier. He also knew the best bridle paths on the Robertses' vast estate.

As October set in, Cara suddenly realized that although galloping up Roly's Hill was fun, she hadn't begun working Lucas toward shows, as she'd promised Stephanie she would. He needed to be schooled and jumped every day.

Cara worried for a week about the best way to do this. She read every horse book she owned on show jumping, trying to figure out a schooling program that would suit Lucas and fit into her hectic work schedule. Luckily Mr. Roberts had put floodlights around a ring for Stephanie, so Cara would be able to continue schooling Lucas through the long winter months when it would get dark right after school.

"Why do you worry so much when you've got it made?" Tansy asked as they walked through the halls to class.

"I know, I know, don't keep telling me," Cara pleaded. "Don't you see that's exactly what's wrong?"

Tansy bit into a pear to the core and shook her head.

"I have a wonderful horse, who lives at a perfect farm, with all expenses paid—I have to live up to it all," Cara said with a sigh.

"Okay, I get it," said Tansy, grinning. "So do you have to get an Olympic gold medal just once a month or does it have to be twice?"

Cara hardly heard her. "You'll go crazy when I tell you this," she began nervously.

"Try me—I'm tough."

"I'm thinking of asking Ms. P. to give me private riding lessons," Cara blurted.

"Ms. P!" Tansy spluttered, dropping her pear on the floor. "You're completely nuts! You just managed to get rid of the old bat."

"She's the best around here," Cara insisted. "She knows more about show jumping than anybody else in the county."

"Oh, I guess," Tansy agreed reluctantly. "But she's so awful to deal with."

4

THE NEXT AFTERNOON CARA SKIPPED HER VISIT TO LUCAS and went to see Ms. P. instead. She found her out in one of the warm-up rings, coaching a tiny girl on a gray Shetland pony. The little girl was overexcited and trying too hard, and she bobbed in the saddle like a rosy apple. Ms. P., holding a lead rope, firmly guided the frisky pony around the field, shouting instructions all the while.

"Don't slouch, Charlotte! Keep your reins down. Hug the pony's sides with your knees. Well done—trot on!"

Cara watched until the lesson came to an end. She vividly remembered her own early days with Ms. P. and her terror of making a mistake. *She's not nearly as bad as she sometimes pretends to be*, Cara thought as Ms. P. smiled reassuringly at the little girl in the saddle.

"That will do it for today. Walk him out awhile, Charlotte," said Ms. P. She looked directly across the field at Cara. "So, what's on your mind?"

27

"May I ask you something? It will only take five minutes," Cara said timidly, most of her old fears returning.

Ms. P. led her into the dusty office and sat behind her ancient desk. Cara slid onto a battered leather sofa that looked more like a huge, beat-up saddle than a piece of furniture.

"How can I help?" Ms. P. asked.

Cara fidgeted. She hadn't seen much of Ms. P. over the summer, although Tansy had kept up her Saturday riding lessons. Tansy had told Cara that Ms. P. sometimes grumbled about Cara's absence, complaining that the minute she trained a good rider, that person inevitably left to ride for somebody else's stable. Cara felt a little guilty about deserting Ms. P.—she *had* given her years of training and encouragement.

"Well . . ." she began nervously, "I just wondered . . . if you might have time to coach me once a week on Lucas?"

Ms. P. stared at her. Then, to Cara's surprise and relief, she smiled warmly.

"I'd be delighted to," she answered. "We'll work over at the Robertses' stable, where we'll have fewer distractions."

"Thank you!" Cara said happily.

"It's going to be expensive, my dear," Ms. P. added. "Can you afford it?"

"Yes," lied Cara. The truth was she could barely afford a lesson every other week, and that would leave her broke for the rest of the month. Still, that wasn't Ms. P.'s problem.

28

"Fine. Then I'll see you Sunday, at two o'clock sharp!" Ms. P. said briskly.

The next Sunday Ms. P. arrived at the Robertses' with guns blazing.

"Do you call that horse groomed?" she snapped as she marched across the stable yard.

"Yes," Cara answered, stung. "I spent half an hour grooming him."

"Humph," sniffed Ms. P. as she circled Lucas. "Since he's not your horse, you'd better not slack off with him."

Cara sighed and waited. After Ms. P. had found fault with everything for a while, she would get down to giving useful advice. "I know I should take extra-special care of him," Cara answered politely.

"All right, then," barked Ms. P., smacking her riding crop against her gleaming leather boots. "Let's get to work."

Cara led Lucas across the stable yard and out into the ring, where jumps had been set up. Lucas seemed to know he was on display and pranced and tossed his silky mane.

Good for him; Ms. P. will get the right impression, Cara thought.

Ms. P. stopped them before the gate to the ring. She ran her hands down Lucas's legs, expertly examining them for any scars or splints. "Clean as they come." She slapped Lucas's rippling hindquarters. "Nothing like a horse with good legs," she pronounced.

Cara, knowing that she rarely gave compliments, glowed with pride.

"He's a fine animal," Ms. P. commented.

Cara stared at her, thunderstruck. In all her years of working at Hunters' Riding School, she had never heard Ms. P. make an openly enthusiastic remark about a horse. That wasn't to say Ms. P. didn't care about her horses, but she was never one to get caught indulging in sentiment.

"You *like* him?" Cara gasped.

"Certainly," said Ms. P. "Now mount up and put him into a collected walk along the fence."

Cara quickly mounted, walked Lucas to the fence, and then pulled back on the reins until his neck arched and his body was poised in a collected walk.

"Hmm," said Ms. P. "Out into an extended walk."

Cara loosened the reins slightly and urged Lucas into a quick walk.

"Posting trot!" the instructor shouted as they rounded the far corner. The lesson on the flat continued for an hour, with Ms. P. drilling Cara through the basics in the grueling manner that Cara remembered so well.

"And now for some jumps," Ms. P. announced. She set up a low cross jump—two poles in an X—separated by a single stride from a small single-rail vertical, followed by two strides to a combination—two verticals separated by a stride. Then she stepped out to the fence and folded her arms.

"Show her, boy," Cara murmured, gathering the reins.

Lucas didn't disappoint her. He sprang over the jumps effortlessly. Because the jumps were so low,

Cara had time to strengthen and correct her position even in midflight.

Then Ms. P. astonished her by setting up a short course of three-foot-six fences.

"Aren't those a little high?" Cara asked nervously.

"Not for Lucas," Ms. P. answered briefly.

Cara could feel Lucas tense as he faced the bigger jumps. "It's the same deal, boy," she said softly. "You've been over much bigger jumps." Still, she was unprepared for his long takeoff over the first jump and ended up sitting deep in the saddle as they sailed over, instead of correctly up in jump position over his neck.

"Push him on; don't just sit there!" bellowed Ms. P. predictably.

Cara found herself using Lucas's ears as indicators of how he viewed the jumps. When they were pricked forward, he was ready to fly, and she just gave him his head and soared with him. As they landed his ears flattened back and she collected him, talking to him as they headed for the next jump.

Ms. P. varied the jumps and made them more challenging as the lesson progressed. Cara began to feel like her body was splitting in two. Muscles she never realized she had throbbed and screamed as she attempted to follow Ms. P.'s numerous commands.

"Speed him up coming into that triple!" she yelled. "Shorten your reins and sit well forward!"

Cara zoomed over the triple—a jump three rails wide—with feet to spare.

"Not too bad!" Ms. P. cried. "More speed and less sitting back next time!"

31

On the next combination Cara forgot to sit back down as Lucas landed and nearly went over his head.

"Get your rear back in that saddle!" Ms. P. yelled. "Concentrate!"

After about an hour, Cara was able to relax enough to work on really improving their performance. Lucas was a wonderful horse to learn on, with his smooth, bold strides and good judgment in taking the jumps.

He's teaching me as much as Ms. P., she thought.

Almost instinctively Cara began to respond to Lucas's every movement until she felt one with him, as if they shared a set of nerves and muscles. She felt elated, as if she'd reached a higher plane of riding than ever before.

"Better!" called Ms. P. "Much better. Dismount!"

The lesson had been so grueling that Cara's legs folded underneath her when she dismounted. She found herself plopping down into the dirt at Lucas's feet. He carefully stepped sideways and nuzzled her hair, as if he wondered what she was doing.

Ms. P. hauled her to her feet and dusted her down.

"I thought that might happen," she said. "Your upper thigh muscles are weak. Still, they'll improve quickly if you practice those jumps every day."

Cara hobbled across the stable yard to Ms. P.'s rusty station wagon.

"I kept the jumps low," Ms. P. remarked as Cara slid into the front seat.

Low? Cara said to herself. *Right; I guess three foot six is just a walk in the park!*

"We'll get them up next time," Ms. P. said, flashing

Cara one of her rare smiles. "Those jumps were child's play for Lucas."

Cara called Tansy later that afternoon to fill her in on her first lesson. "The height of the jumps wasn't the only thrill," Cara told her. "It was doing them with Lucas. It was as if he wanted to teach me and to be doing them with me."

The next day, although she could hardly walk, Cara was back in the saddle, putting Lucas through his paces and reviewing their lesson. She set up the same first course of three-foot jumps that Ms. P. had, with a single stride between the first and the second jump and a double stride between the second and third jumps.

"Let's get them perfect," she said to Lucas.

Every day after that, she varied their practice work so that Lucas wouldn't get bored and lose his concentration. But by the end of the week she decided that they both needed a change from schooling.

"Let's ride Roly's Hill!" Cara whispered to Lucas as they cantered down the bridle path behind the Robertses' house. Sharing her eagerness, Lucas accelerated beneath her and thundered up the path, brushing trees and bushes as he charged up the hill onto the crest. They stood there together, watching the sunset paint the puffy thunderheads crimson and gold. Cara sighed deeply and leaned down against Lucas's warm neck.

"I"m so happy," she said softly. Lucas tossed his head, as if to say that he was, too.

*   *   *

By Sunday Cara was keenly anticipating her next jumping lesson with Ms. P., but the instructor had other plans for her.

"We'll concentrate on your flat work," she announced.

Flat work was the last thing Cara had expected. Seeing her expression, Ms. P. said, "You can't jump Lucas all the time or he'll get bored. Then you won't have a jumper; you'll have a stable nag."

If it's good for Lucas, it's got to be good for me, Cara thought. "Okay," she said.

"Let's look at the way he approaches the jumps," said Ms. P., smacking her riding crop against her boot. "That's just as important as the actual jump."

They worked for half an hour on Lucas's walk-to-canter transition.

"Cara, get him off the *wrong lead!*" Ms. P. cried. "And for crying out loud, sit deeper in the saddle." Cara stretched her legs down and around Lucas, convinced that her toes would meet underneath his belly. Painful as it was, the improved position seemed to be what Ms. P. wanted. She let them make an entire circuit of the ring without comment.

"His neck's a little stiff," she observed. "Let's do some suppling exercises." She instructed Cara to canter Lucas in a sixty-foot circle. "Now get him to bend!" she called. "Really push him with your inside leg." Cara did as she was told and immediately noticed how soft and balanced he became.

"Excellent!" Ms. P. cried. "Now decrease your circle to forty-five feet."

34

This was much harder. Cara had to get Lucas perfectly collected before she felt that same even, balanced movement.

"Very good," encouraged Ms. P. "Now let's see if you can decrease the circle to thirty feet."

Lucas's ears flicked back as Cara tightened the reins. He responded beautifully, shortening his stride and leaning smoothly into the circle. His enthusiastic performance made Cara try even harder herself.

By the end of the lesson they could canter perfectly in a thirty-, forty-five-, or sixty-foot circle, and Lucas was bending much better, particularly his back and neck.

"All right, that's enough for now," said Ms. P. "You've both worked hard."

"And I thought Lucas was completely supple even before this," said Cara thoughtfully. "That's weird."

"No horse is," Ms. P. replied. "Every competition horse regularly needs to stretch and soften up." She rubbed Lucas's soft nose. "You worked well, Mr. Lucas," she said. "Do you feel good about that?"

Lucas shook his head and bumped her hand, expecting at least one carrot.

"I don't feel so great, even if he does," said Cara, laughing. "I almost had my legs touching under him."

Ms. P. smiled slightly. "It's only pain," she said. "And the way you two look together, it will be worth it in the end."

Cara beamed. Suddenly the persistent throbbing in her calves seemed unimportant.

"Untack him and give him a reward," Ms. P. instructed. "I'll see you next week."

Cara dismounted, barely able to keep her legs from bowing her to the ground again.

"You'll be able to tie yourself in knots by the time Ms. P. gets finished with you," Joseph remarked slyly as he watched Cara limp across the stable yard.

"I thought I was in good shape until Ms. P. started turning me inside out," Cara said, wincing as she pulled Lucas's girth loose. Her arms hurt too, she discovered. Joseph took pity on her and carried the saddle into the tack room.

"Well, you're both looking the better for the workouts," he said encouragingly. "And the jumping's coming on just fine."

"Yes, and it's only pain anyway," Cara said with a sigh.

After school each day, Cara practiced her flat work and jumping, glad of the luxury of Mr. Roberts's floodlights on the dark autumn afternoons. Through the damp November and a sharp, frosty December, Ms. P. laid out a number of short courses for Cara: different kinds of combinations and a wall.

"You've put in enough ground work," Ms. P. said. "Now it's time to take a trip around some fences."

As she and Cara walked the different courses Ms. P. talked her through them. "Collect Lucas quickly after a fence and bring him to the right pace for the next one. Line him up straight coming into each fence so that he's balanced at the takeoff point."

Cara, as always, felt lucky to be riding Lucas. He

could effortlessly lengthen or shorten his gait coming up to a fence, giving a choice of strides on the way to every one. Cara knew he was both patient and giving with her. Although these fences were smaller than any Stephanie would have tackled with him, and a lot of the schooling was repetitive, he still put all he had into each jump.

"He's an excellent horse," Ms. P. said after he and Cara had completed one of her short courses without so much as wobbling a pole. "I think it's time we rewarded him."

Cara nodded, assuming Ms. P. meant carrots. Ms. P.'s next words were a shock.

"How about a trip out to Channings?"

"Channings?" Cara gasped. It was one of the local show-jumping competitions that Ms. P.'s best students regularly attended.

"Certainly. It'll be a challenge for both of you, and just what he needs," she added, stroking Lucas's satin neck. "An intelligent horse like him will eventually get bored with just workouts."

Keeping Lucas lively and interested had been preoccupying Cara too. "When is the show?" she asked.

"This Sunday. I'll enter you and arrange for a van with Mr. Roberts. I'll see you then." Ms. P. gave Lucas a final pat and strode off to her car, leaving Cara with her mouth open. Lucas nudged her arm.

"Sorry, boy," she murmured absently. "I've got bigger things on my mind other than your dinner!"

5

CHANNINGS WAS EXACTLY WHAT MS. P. HAD PREDICTED—A
challenge. Cara was entered for the Discovery
class, a solid round of three-foot-six fences. When
she got to the show and checked the program, she
found that Ms. P. had entered her for the Foxhunter
class too.

"Those fences will be three foot nine," gasped
Cara, her heart thumping.

"Nothing ventured, nothing gained," replied Ms.
P. with an authoritative smack of her crop.

Nervous butterflies might be whizzing around
Cara's stomach, but Lucas was bombproof. As he
backed down the ramp out of the van he threw up his
head and sniffed the air, then whinnied eagerly to the
other horses.

"Okay, Lucas, we all know you're wonderful, but
some people don't yet," said Cara, laughing.

"He's always this way at shows," Joseph said,

smiling too. "He just can't wait to get in there and impress everybody."

Joseph took care of Lucas while Cara walked the course for the Discovery class, measuring the distance between the jumps and carefully planning their ride. Then she mounted up and waited outside the ring for their names to be called. Lucas stood quietly, ignoring the frantic bustle of horses, riders, and grooms around him. Cara took her cue from him, using the time remaining before their round to center her mind on the course.

"Erin's Luck, ridden by Cara Zol, owned by Lionel Roberts!"

When Cara heard Lucas's show name called, she rode him through the gate to the ring. She realized she was shaking all over, and when she tried to say a few reassuring words to Lucas, all that came out was a squeak.

Lucas approached the first jump, striding perfectly to takeoff. Cara was the novice, holding her breath and even closing her eyes with excitement as they took off. Lucas cleared jump after jump. After the fourth fence she was back in control, urging him on around the corners, then checking his stride to straighten him and changing his lead with each change of direction.

Lucas was the only horse with a completely clean round, and they won the class. Cara rode out of the ring, her face ablaze with happiness.

"Well done!" cried Ms. P.

"He was absolutely wonderful," Cara said, still

trying to catch her breath.

"He certainly was," agreed Ms. P., rubbing Lucas's elegant ears. "And you did fine too," she added.

Cara felt tears sting the back of her eyes. "Thank you," she said.

But Ms. P. didn't linger on sentiment. "Come along now," she said, pointing at Lucas's heaving flanks. "Cool him off before the Foxhunter class."

Cara began to smile as she watched Ms. P. stomp off and bellow at a gaggle of her giggling Pony Club stars. "Hurry up! What do you think this is—a circus?" she shouted at them.

The girls scattered, shooting terrified looks over their shoulders at Ms. P., exactly as Cara would have done only a few months before. It seemed a long time ago. Ms. P. was one of her biggest supporters now.

She's interested in Lucas, Cara thought. But she knew it was more than that. Ms. P. had ambitions for her, too—big ambitions.

"Let's hope I turn out as well as you," she whispered to Lucas, slipping a halter over his bridle to walk him.

The Foxhunter class didn't go nearly as well as the first class. The higher jumps made Cara nervous going in, and she lost it completely on their approach to a solid, forbidding brick wall. She hesitated in cueing Lucas on his takeoff, and his late pop close to the jump brought down the top section of bricks.

"Won your first class, anyway," Joseph said consolingly as Cara loaded Lucas in the van after the show.

40

Cara nodded happily. She was delighted with her one blue ribbon from the Discovery class. "I can't wait for the next show," she said.

"There'll be a lot more," Joseph said, stowing her saddle in the storage compartment of the van.

Mr. Roberts came out to meet them as they drove into the stable yard.

"Excellent!" he said, smiling as Cara attached the blue ribbon to Lucas's halter. "Just like old times." He slapped Lucas's neck lightly.

Cara stopped dead, suddenly remembering that Lucas had done all of this before. The Channings show had been wonderfully exciting for her, but it was just an old rerun for Lucas and Mr. Roberts. Worse—this time a year ago, Stephanie would have been jumping Lucas in really big shows.

"Thanks for putting up with a beginner," she whispered gratefully to Lucas as she spread fresh straw in his stall for the night. Lucas looked at her for a moment with his soft dark eyes, then lowered his head so that she could rub his ears.

"Are you talking to me, missy?" Joseph teased as he passed by on his way to the feed room.

"No, to Lucas."

"Everybody's got to start somewhere, you know," Joseph said as he mixed Lucas's supper. Lucas abruptly lifted his head and began pacing his stall, searching through the wire mesh for signs of his dinner.

"Just you look here," said Joseph, coming up to the

stall with Lucas's black rubber bucket. "Sweet feed and oats, and for dessert—" He held up a big, ripe red apple. "Got one for you, too," he said to Cara, tossing her another apple. "Well done!"

Led by Lucas, tutored by Ms. P., and encouraged by Mr. Roberts, Cara made rapid progress with her jumping. As the long, dark winter months set in she spent every spare minute at the stable, training under the floodlights, determined to put as much effort into working Lucas as he did into teaching her. In mid-December, Ms. P. dropped her bombshell.

"I've entered you in the show-jumping classes at one of the Barracks shows on January 1," she announced.

Cara nearly fainted. The Barracks series of shows were big events—definitely not for amateurs.

"But—Do you really think . . ." Cara stammered.

"I do. Lucas is ready for it!" barked Ms. P.

Yes, Cara thought. *But what about* me?

"Better check with Mr. Roberts before you get too carried away," Mrs. Zol advised when Cara told her about the show. "Stephanie will be home for Christmas. She'll want to ride Lucas too."

Stephanie! How could she have forgotten *her*? Cara had been so absorbed in riding and jumping Lucas that she hadn't even thought about Stephanie for weeks now. Of course she'd be back for the holidays—and of course she'd want to ride Lucas. After all, he was her horse.

"Maybe Stephanie would like to enter the show,"

Cara suggested to Mr. Roberts.

"I doubt that." He laughed. "After three months of hanging out in Santa Barbara, she'll be in no shape to ride, believe me. You just keep up the good work and Stephanie will be delighted." Cara sighed with relief, but she couldn't put Stephanie out of her mind after that.

"I'd completely forgotten about Stephanie," she confessed to Tansy in the school library the next day. "It was like she didn't exist and Lucas belonged to me, only me," she added.

"Shhh!" hissed the librarian. Cara lowered her voice.

"Getting Lucas was like having all my dreams came true," she whispered. "So Stephanie won't want to show him over the vacation. But what if she comes back here to live?" Cara's voice trembled. "What if she takes him to Santa Barbara?"

"She probably will come back eventually—Virginia's a neat place, especially for riding," said Tansy.

Cara nodded and looked even glummer.

"Come on, Cara, you've got at least three years before that happens," said Tansy reassuringly. "Make the most of it!"

This time the librarian half rose from her chair. Cara and Tansy bent their heads studiously over their notebooks.

"Worry about Stephanie later," Tansy whispered.

As Christmas approached, Mr. Roberts looked increasingly gloomy. He seldom visited the stable for his customary chat with Lucas. In fact, Cara hardly saw him at all.

"What's the matter with Mr. Roberts?" she asked her mother.

"He's worried about Stephanie," said Mrs. Zol. "She's got a boyfriend."

"So what? Millions of girls at college have boyfriends. Even half the girls in my class are dating."

"She's spending the entire vacation with him," said Mrs. Zol.

"She's not coming home at all for Christmas?" Cara was shocked.

"No," said her mother. "It's no wonder Mr. Roberts is upset. Although if Stephanie doesn't come home, I think he'll visit her in California just so he sees something of her."

Cara frowned. She had heard Mr. Roberts talk about Stephanie every day, at least twice a day, for the past three months.

"It's mean of her not to come home, boyfriend or not," she fumed.

"Well, boys have a funny effect on girls sometimes," said Mrs. Zol with an infuriating smile.

"I won't ever let boys be more important to me than horses," Cara replied firmly.

The next day she got a Christmas card from Stephanie, raving about her new boyfriend, Dan, who was from Los Angeles. She barely mentioned Lucas in one sentence.

"I just don't see how she can give up Lucas for

some boy," Cara told Tansy as they lined up for lunch in the school cafeteria.

"What do you care?" Tansy asked. "The less she's around, the more time you get with Lucas. You'll need it too, with the Barracks show coming up."

"Yeah, I guess I hadn't thought about it like that," Cara admitted.

"Think positive," Tansy said. "And while we're on the subject, *some* boys are almost as interesting as horses."

"Not Paul Knight, your famous science partner?" Cara asked with a grin.

"*Especially* the famous Paul Knight!" Tansy replied, giggling.

6

CARA TRIED HARD TO CONCENTRATE ON THE CHRISTMAS celebrations that year, for her family's sake, but twinkling Christmas trees, roast turkey, and even presents were the very last thing on her mind. Every minute away from Lucas and the stable was an agony. As she pounded around the shopping malls, her mind shut out the sound of piped Christmas carols and focused only on water jumps and triple oxers.

But Mike was wild with excitement over Christmas. "What are you getting Mom and Dad?" he asked her every day.

"Well—" Cara started, and got no further.

"How about a giraffe or a helicopter?" Mike suggested.

Cara laughed, but quickly came back to reality. "I'm totally broke," she said. "I can afford only small presents this year." Seeing the disappointment on her brother's face, she added, "We could make Mom and

Dad something really nice instead."

"A giraffe," said Mike, instantly cheering up.

"Okay, great, a giraffe," Cara agreed. "But you've got to help me cut it out and sew it."

Finally, two days before Christmas, Cara went to the large shopping mall nearby with her dad. Using the little money she had left, she bought her mother a pair of pretty earrings, her dad a new pen while he wasn't looking, Tansy a paperback on show jumping, and Mike a toy helicopter.

"That's it," she said. "I'm all finished."

"What about you, sweetheart?" asked Mr. Zol as they pushed through the crowded mall.

"Me?" Cara asked, surprised.

"Christmas, remember?" her dad teased.

"Oh." Cara stopped short. Two frantic shoppers almost ran her over. "Honestly, I don't want anything now that I've got Lucas!" she said.

"You and that horse," said Mr. Zol with a fond smile. "Sometimes I think he's more important to you than any person."

"No, he isn't," Cara answered, but sometimes she wondered herself.

To Cara's astonishment, Ms. P. gave her a free riding lesson as a Christmas present. Her own present for the instructor, a scarf decorated with galloping horses, seemed insignificant beside it.

"I . . . I don't know what to say," Cara mumbled.

"Then don't say anything," replied Ms. P. briskly. "If you keep working hard and do well at the Barracks show, that will be thanks enough."

47

On Christmas Eve, as Cara settled Lucas down for the night, she sang "Away in a Manger" and "Rudolf the Red-Nosed Reindeer" to him. Lucas occasionally lipped her jacket as she sang and obviously enjoyed the attention. He stamped one hoof when she'd finished.

"Does that mean you want an encore?" she asked. Although it could only have been a coincidence, at that moment Lucas bobbed his head. Cara sang "Hark, the Herald Angels Sing," her voice echoing across the dark, frosty yard.

"Merry Christmas, buddy," she whispered as she left. "I've got something for you in the morning!"

Christmas morning was full of surprises. Underneath the tree were two hefty presents for Cara, and two little ones.

"Merry Christmas, honey," said her mother, kissing her. Cara quickly opened one of the big gifts. Slowly she pulled out of the wrapping a gorgeous black show-jumping coat. The next big package contained cream jodhpurs.

"Mom! Dad!" she cried. "I can't believe it." In the smaller packages were an elegant cravat and a silver cravat pin Mike had bought her, with a horse jumping over a five-bar gate.

"Maybe the pin will give you good luck, Cara," Mike said, grinning with excitement at her pleasure.

"Thank you," she answered, giving him a hug. "I'm sure it will."

After they had a huge Christmas lunch, Cara's mom drove her over to the stables. The house was strangely dark and silent.

"I hope Mr. Roberts is having a good time in Los Angeles," Cara said.

"I'm sure he is," said her mother.

Fear suddenly clutched Cara's heart. "Mom, do you think there's any chance that he might *stay* there?" she asked.

"What, move away from Virginia? No, sweetie. He can't—his business is here," her mother answered.

Cara let out a long sigh of relief. "Good," she said.

Somehow the anxious thought stayed with her, though. She had to keep reminding herself that Lucas wasn't hers. She could never be sure how long their wonderful times together would last.

Joseph had turned Lucas out that morning. Kicking up his heels, he trotted across the frosty paddock when he saw the car drive up.

"Here comes my guy! Merry Christmas!" Cara called. She ran up to Lucas with her arms behind her back. She had tied up a whole bag of carrots with a red ribbon for Lucas as a Christmas present. The big horse sniffed first one arm, then the other.

"Go on, you choose," she said, laughing at his excited expression. When he nuzzled her left arm, Cara held up a carrot. "And for dessert," she said, holding out her right hand with a sugar cube.

"I swear that horse understands every word you say," said Mrs. Zol with a laugh.

"That's what I keep telling her," said Joseph, coming up behind them.

"Merry Christmas," said Cara, giving Joseph a hug. She had made Joseph a big chocolate cake, decorated with nuts and cherries. He beamed when she handed it to him, and Cara suddenly regretted that she hadn't showed up earlier. She remembered that Joseph lived with his old invalid mother in a house on the Robertses' estate. They might have enjoyed some company.

Lucas seemed to think so too. Nudging Cara to one side, he wriggled in between her and Mrs. Zol, putting his nose on Joseph's shoulder. Huffing quietly, he sniffed Joseph's ear. Joseph laughed, then opened the cake box. Lucas watched, intrigued.

"This has got to be one of the most beautiful cakes I've ever seen," said Joseph, clearly touched. "Stay right there—I've got a little something for you." He hurried off to the tack room and came back with a tin box.

"It's kind of old, but I thought it might interest you," he said a little shyly.

Cara opened the box. Inside was an old pair of silver spurs. They were delicately engraved with a filigree motif and Joseph's initials.

"They're beautiful!" she exclaimed.

"I wore them a long time ago," Joseph explained, sounding self-conscious. "Thought you might like them, though Lucas won't," he added hastily.

"They're so pretty," Cara said, holding them up to the glinting wintry sun.

"Can't think of a better person to hand 'em on to," Joseph finished gruffly. "And I've got something for you, boy," he added, holding up a big red apple. "Christmas wouldn't be Christmas without you!"

Cara took some time from her training for big, long family meals, skating with Tansy, and even a school dance, but by the end of all the feasting and celebrating she was in a fever to get back to intense training with Lucas. The Barracks show was less than a week away. Ms. P. varied the jump heights—three foot six, three foot nine, sometimes four feet. Luckily she usually kept the jumps under four feet, since jumping that high always gave Cara an attack of nerves. But even at four feet Lucas was so solid underneath her, and Ms. P talked her through the jumps so expertly, that they flew perfectly over almost every jump. Lucas actually performed better, if that was possible, in the frosty air. Even Ms. P. was pleased.

"Excellent, excellent!" she shouted after their last practice in the icy cold ring before the show. "The ground is a bit too hard for him, but he's giving it his all, aren't you, handsome?"

Cara hid a smile. She still couldn't believe hard-as-nails Ms. P. had a soft side.

"No New Year's Eve party nonsense," Ms. P. advised. "Get a good night's sleep."

Cara nodded. She had no intention of partying the night away.

"Oh, come on, Cara," Tansy said crossly on the phone that night. "Sure, you're in training, but it's New Year's Eve! You're not going to even one party?"

"Nope," Cara said firmly. "Don't forget; I have to be up at dawn."

"Everybody will be having fun but you," Tansy said.

"Lucas is fun," Cara pointed out.

"Party pooper."

"Another time," Cara promised, her thoughts already back on the show.

7

CARA DID GO TO BED EARLY THAT NIGHT, ALTHOUGH SHE had trouble sleeping, with all the celebrations going on up and down the street. She was too nervous and excited to sleep much anyway. Occasionally she would doze off, then wake with a start, terrified that she'd slept through the alarm.

Her dad drove her to the stables at five the next morning. Bleary-eyed, he left her in the icy yard with Joseph. "Good luck, sweetheart, we'll be thinking of you," he called as he disappeared down the dark drive. Mr. Zol worked as much overtime as he could on weekends, which gave him little free time to watch Cara compete.

Joseph smiled at Cara. "Good to know I'm not the only person up in the world," he said.

Cara found Lucas dozing on his deep straw bed.

"Wake up, buddy; we've got a big day ahead," she called softly. Lucas quickly got his feet under him and shook himself. Cara gave him an early breakfast, then crosstied him in the aisle and started to groom him.

"You've got to look your handsomest," she said, briskly brushing his back. Joseph had recently given him a hunter clip for the winter, which left the top part of his coat thick and warm but his legs and underbelly sleekly shaved so that he wouldn't get too hot jumping. "We can't have Merlin's Wand outshining you," she added.

Merlin's Wand belonged to Vicki Wolfe, another of Ms. P's star pupils. Cara had ridden with her over the years and was still slightly in awe of her. Vicki would certainly be at the Barracks show with her speedy Arab gray.

It took Cara a long time to carefully plait up Lucas's long mane and tail. Bits of hair kept sticking out or getting caught in the rubber bands, but she persevered. By the time she'd finished, Lucas seemed to know exactly where he was going. His ears were up, his eyes were bright, and he kept nudging her excitedly. Cara laughed at his impatience.

"Cool it," she said. "I'm excited too, but there's a lot more I have to get done. Let's wrap your legs so you don't hurt yourself on the trip."

The wretched leg wraps nearly drove her crazy. She tried to do them too fast, and they unraveled and flopped around his hooves.

"Sorry, boy," she apologized as she began wrapping for the third time. "I guess I'm a little nervous."

By the time she'd finished all the preparations, it was after seven and Cara was in a sweat. She'd

54

thrown off her coat and sweater to work in jeans and a T-shirt, hardly aware of the frosty morning and frozen water buckets.

"You going to the show in that outfit, missy?" teased Joseph.

"No," Cara answered, wiping sweat from her forehead.

"Well, at least one of you looks mighty handsome," said Joseph, standing back to admire Lucas. The big chestnut did indeed look handsome. Plaited up, groomed down, and swathed in a thick red traveling blanket, he was immaculate.

"I'll load him while you get changed," said Joseph tactfully.

Grateful that Lucas was a dream horse to load, Cara dashed into the tack room and quickly changed into her new riding coat and jodhpurs. Although she couldn't see the entire effect, the clothes make her feel good, like a professional. Straightening her new cravat as best she could without a mirror, she fingered Mike's silver pin.

"Bring me luck," she whispered; then, straightening her shoulders, she joined Joseph in the cab of the horse van.

As they drove the fifty miles to the Barracks show, a pale winter sun rose, lighting the edges of the slate-gray sky to a soft fuschia. Excited as she was, the combination of the restless night she had spent and the warm van made her eyelids slowly droop. In no time Cara was fast asleep, with her head pressed against the window. She awoke with a start.

"Hold on," said Joseph, deftly steering the van over deeply rutted tracks.

They parked beside a long line of horse vans and began unloading Lucas. The second he was down the ramp, he threw back his head and neighed shrilly, as if to say, I'm here!

"They see you, silly!" Cara said with a laugh. She helped Joseph tack up Lucas, then dashed to the show office to check the exact times of her classes. There she found Ms. P. and Vicki Wolfe. Vicki was impeccably dressed from head to toe.

"Hi," both girls said warily.

As Cara read the show program, she felt Vicki's eyes raking up and down her, checking out her riding clothes. *Probably figuring out what they cost*, Cara thought. Her heart sank as she read along the program and discovered that she and Vicki were entered in the same classes.

Ms. P. broke the tension.

"Well," she said cheerfully, "looks like we're in for a busy day, girls."

Cara smiled politely. She wondered if it wasn't totally accidental that she and Vicki would be competing. Could Ms. P. be pitting them against each other?

Lucas can win anything, Cara thought. Suddenly confident, she held out her hand to Vicki. "Good luck," she said.

Vicki smiled warmly. "Good luck to you too," she replied.

Lucas's welcoming whinny as she returned to the van made Cara even more confident.

"Hi, buddy," she whispered into his mane. "Ready to show everybody just how great you are?" Lucas pawed the ground like a warhorse.

"Okay," she said, mounting up. "Let's go for it!"

Her first class was a course of three-foot-six jumps, which she and Lucas cleared with confidence and ease. They won the class on the first round.

The second class, however, was a course of three-foot-nine jumps. Cara knew she and Lucas could handle the jumps just fine, as long as nerves didn't get the better of her. But when her name was called and "Erin's Luck" boomed around the show ring, Cara's hands began to shake.

Ms. P. must have noticed her sudden panic. She said in her briskest voice, "Don't lose your nerve now, Cara. Remember, this is a team effort!"

Cara gritted her teeth and tried to focus solely on the course and Lucas. Breaking into an even canter, Lucas took the first oxer—a spread of two parallel rails—with ease, landing lightly and responding to Cara's hands on the reins as she turned him to face the next jump, a gate. Her spirits suddenly rose as she felt him open up, instinctively anticipating the next jump. The rush of his soaring liftoff and the thrill of a clear landing made her blood pound in her ears. She was almost sorry when it was all over.

"Clear round." The announcer's voice echoed around the ring as she trotted out.

"Super, boy! We've won two classes!" she told Lucas, leaning forward to rub his ears.

"Great job!" Ms. P. boomed. Cara grinned tri-

57

umphantly. Two clear rounds was far more than she had dared hope for.

"Walk him out," Ms. P. instructed. "We're not done here yet." Cara stared at her, puzzled. "We only entered two classes. Didn't we?" she added warily.

"Why not give the Stakes a try?"

The Barracks show Stakes! Cara nearly fell off Lucas's back. "Every jump in that class is four feet!" she squeaked.

"You've jumped four feet many times in the ring," Ms. P. insisted. "Lucas can easily jump that high." She looked at Cara and seemed to read her mind. "Yes, I know the ring isn't the same as the Barracks show ring. But if you have the guts to enter the Stakes, it could be your ticket to the regional finals in Culpeper."

Cara's nervousness disappeared in a flash. The regional finals! Only the top horses in this area of Virginia were invited to show there.

Cara drew a deep breath. "Okay. We'll do it," she answered.

"I knew you would," said Ms. P. slyly. "I entered you last week."

She walked away, leaving Cara staring after her. *Thanks a bunch for asking me,* Cara thought. But she knew that if Ms. P. had asked her earlier, she would never have said yes. Now she didn't have time to worry—the Stakes were the first class after lunch.

Fifteen competitors had entered, including Vicki on Merlin's Wand. Cara was fifth.

"Number thirty-three, Erin's Luck, ridden by Cara Zol, owned by Mr. Lionel Roberts."

Cara swallowed hard and pressed her knees into Lucas's sides.

"This is it, beautiful," she murmured into his pricked ears.

Lucas tossed his head, proudly shaking his braided gold mane.

Cara cantered him around the ring in a preliminary circle, taking deep breaths, then headed Lucas for the first fence. The first fence was a welcoming, fairly simple vertical—two rails one on top of the other—followed by a big combination. Although she was aware of the clock ticking away, Cara knew better than to blow their chances by thundering at every jump in sight, risking a knockdown and the resulting four-fault penalty. Pulling Lucas up, she approached a four-foot wall just off a turn. Lucas collected his strides into a perfect, even rhythm. As the wall blazed red and white before them, Cara kept her focus, straight through Lucas's ears, and cleared it with a foot to spare.

The drop down made her stomach lurch, and she could feel Lucas lose the rhythm of his stride beneath her. She pulled him in again, murmuring, "Easy boy . . . steady." She let him out for the next vertical, which he breezed over. The water jump loomed before them, much wider than she'd anticipated, but Lucas balanced himself, found the correct position, and floated over it.

"Wonderful, boy," Cara murmured, her heart pounding. A combination and some vertical planks were the next jumps, followed by the final jump: a

59

huge triple oxer, three rails wide, that could be successfully taken only if their approach and speed were perfect. Cara shortened her reins, waited for Lucas to find his stride, then urged him on with her legs. She felt the soaring power of his liftoff and the air rush past her as they cleared the spread.

"Clear round for Erin's Luck." The commentator's voice boomed around the ring as Cara slumped onto Lucas's hot neck, shaking with relief.

"You're my hero!" she whispered to him.

It didn't seem fair to make Lucas hang around in the warm-up ring, where the contestants took practice jumps on their horses before the classes, so she trotted him outside, across the fields and away from the crowds. Once they had left the frantic pace of the show, both of them calmed down. Lucas sniffed the frosty air as Cara thoughtfully walked him along the hedges, going over the course and silently celebrating her good fortune. After ten minutes she walked him back to the warm-up ring, where Vicki was waiting for her.

"We're both through to the jump-off," she announced.

"Great!" Cara replied, sincerely glad of Vicki's company. Vicki had not done well in the first two classes they had both entered. "Let's walk the course together."

Leaving Lucas with Joseph, Cara inspected the new course. Roughly half the number of jumps from the previous round were left, all tightly arranged on a smaller, tougher course.

"These turns are deadly," Vicki said, expertly striding out the distances between the jumps.

"And higher," gasped Cara, staring at the intimidating final jump.

"I wish I had wings," Vicki said with a laugh.

Only seven had made it through to the jump-off: Cara, Vicki, a teenage boy, two men, and two women. This time Cara was the last to go. She watched the others, her heart beginning to pound again. Their speeds were very fast, and, if competitors had clear rounds, the fastest speed would decide the winner. As Cara headed for the show ring there were only two clear rounds, one of them Vicki's.

"Good luck, Cara," she said as they passed in the ring.

Oddly, Cara wasn't at all nervous. After such a spectacular morning, she was on a high. In one day she'd achieved more than she could ever have hoped for—whatever came next was going to be fun.

When the starting bell sounded, her mind went icy clear, and she was able to focus her attention easily on only Lucas and the jumps. Later she realized their speed had been good, but during the class they seemed to be moving in slow motion while she saw everything around them—the jumps, the white board fence of the ring, the applauding crowd—with perfect clarity.

Rising and falling with Lucas, gathering him in on the tightest of turns, Cara held her breath, waiting for the final jump: the enormous triple oxer. She gave Lucas his head, and he found his stride. She leaned forward into the jump. With a *whoosh* of cold air, they were clear.

Then she heard a dull thud. Oh, no! They couldn't have knocked down a pole after such a perfect takeoff and landing. Cara turned quickly in the saddle to look. The spread was still intact!

Maybe we just wobbled it, she thought.

"Clear round. Erin's Luck. Fifty-eight seconds," called the commentator.

"Fifty-eight seconds!" Cara gasped. "I don't believe it."

"You won! You won!" yelled Ms. P. and Vicki as she trotted out of the ring. Cara swung out of the saddle and threw her arms around Lucas's neck.

"Oh, thank you, thank you," she cried against his mane. Then she turned and did something she would never have thought possible—she hugged Ms. P. "Thank you, too," she said. She felt like kissing everybody in the ring.

"Here are the results of the Stakes class," the judge's voice crackled over the loudspeaker. "In first place number thirty-three, Erin's Luck, fifty-eight seconds, ridden by Cara Zol. In second place number twenty, Merlin's Wand, sixty-four seconds, ridden by Vicki Wolfe. Third, number seventy-three, Bronze Head, seventy-two seconds, ridden by Jonathan Ward. These three now advance to the Culpeper regional finals on March 21."

Cara and Vicki hugged each other tight.

"We made it!" they yelled, jumping up and down with excitement.

Ms. P. smiled proudly. "You both deserve your success—you've worked hard for it," she said.

Praise from Ms. P. was a perfect ending to a dazzling day, Cara thought, and went home happier than she could ever remember being.

Much later that night, as snow fell in soft drifts outside, she settled Lucas in his warm stall. Contented after a bran mash supper, he nudged her for his usual carrots.

"We're going places, buddy," she told him as he crunched his way through treats. "Anything's possible . . ." she added, staring out at the swirling snow with a dreamy, faraway look in her dark blue eyes.

A week later Mr. Roberts returned from Los Angeles and announced that Lucas was for sale.

8

"WHY, WHY—*WHY*?" CARA SOBBED.

"Honey," said her mother, patiently repeating the story that Cara now knew backward and forward, "Lucas is Stephanie's horse. If she decides to sell him, for *whatever* reason, you don't have a say in the matter."

The very word *sell* let loose another flood of tears. "How could she?" Cara raged, the tears streaming down her face.

Mrs. Zol calmly continued, "Sweetheart, I know it's hard for you to understand, but believe me, the sooner you come to terms with the reality of the situation, the better it will be for you."

"But Lucas!" Cara wept. "Where will he go?"

"Shh," murmured Mrs. Zol. "You'll make yourself sick if you carry on like this."

At that moment Cara didn't care if she lived or died. Life without Lucas would be like a nightmare.

"Something will happen," she kept saying to herself. "Something *will* keep Mr. Roberts from selling Lucas." Maybe there was a chance she could persuade him not to sell Lucas. Maybe she could put it to him that Stephanie would be interested in horses again once she fell out of love with Dan.

"You're just fooling yourself, honey," her mother said after Cara poured out her plan. "Lucas is going to be sold—and that's a fact."

"He can't be sold. I won't let him!" Cara said to herself through clenched teeth. "Just wait till I see Mr. Lionel Roberts."

Mr. Roberts was clearly avoiding both her and Lucas. A whole week went by and he never once showed up at the stable, which he used to visit every day. Summoning up all her nerve, Cara went to the house to see him. When he opened the door, she was shocked by the change in him. His usual cheerful expression had been replaced by a hard, grim look she had never seen before.

"I'm sorry, Cara. There's nothing I can do," he said when she'd finished her speech. "Stephanie's made up her mind. She's completely infatuated with that young man, Dan." Cara saw a flicker of dislike cross Mr. Roberts's face. "She's adamant about settling down in California when she finishes college, and she wants to sell Lucas now, while he's in peak condition."

"Maybe she'll change her mind," Cara suggested, but hope was fading fast.

Mr. Roberts shook his head. "Not a chance. Horses are a thing of the past in her new life."

Cara hung her head so that he wouldn't see the tears in her eyes.

"I know," Mr. Roberts said. "I'll miss him too."

Cara looked into his sad, careworn face and realized she wasn't the only one suffering.

"I'm sorry," she mumbled, and hurried away before either of them could burst into tears.

The advertisement went into the local paper and some national riding magazines at the beginning of February. Every day was torture for Cara—would it be her last with Lucas?

During Lucas's grooming sessions she no longer chatted to him or made jokes. Now she was sad or even despondent, often resting her head against his neck and weeping into his mane. Lucas sensed the change in her and seemed confused. He would gently nudge her hair, as if to say, I love you too. He gave her strength, but the nagging, aching fear wouldn't go away.

"It would almost be better if I didn't see him," she confessed to Tansy one day after school. "He's so gentle and trusting. Every time he looks at me, I feel like he's trying to ask me something. I know it sounds dumb, but I'm sure he knows what's going on."

"He's a smart horse," Tansy agreed. "Gee, Cara, I'm so sorry. If only you could keep him."

"If only . . ." Cara answered.

All the joy had gone out of visiting the stables. Joseph moped around with a face as long as a fiddle.

"I just can't imagine that old horse not being around here," he admitted to Cara. "He's a bright spot in every day."

Cara nodded. Lucas had brought them all together, making them happy for months now. The thought of him not being in the paddock, grazing in the sunshine, or in the stable yard, watching Joseph mucking out his stall while she tacked him up for a ride on Roly's Hill, was unbearable.

Lucas's spirits had sunk too. He became subdued and slightly edgy.

"He's not jumping as well as he was," complained Ms. P. one wintry Sunday afternoon. "Neither are you, but that's understandable," she added gently.

"I'm sorry," Cara said, her voice choked with tears.

Ms. P. whacked her whip crossly against her boots. "It's such a shame," she said, half to herself. "Just when you both were doing so well." She stared at Cara's unhappy face and tired eyes. "You must try not to take it so hard. He might be sold locally; you never know. I'd like him myself, but he'd be wasted at the school." Cara cringed. She couldn't imagine which would be worse: Lucas going away altogether or Lucas at Hunters' Riding School, ridden by every kid in the neighborhood.

A few days later Mr. Roberts dropped by the stable and said, "A neighbor's coming to see Lucas this afternoon."

Cara's heart thumped. She flushed and said, "Neighbor?" There weren't any for miles around.

"Mrs. Deneuve," he explained. "She bought the old farmhouse down the road just before Christmas. She's looking for a horse for her daughters to ride." He turned abruptly and left the stable yard, obviously not wishing to discuss the matter further.

"Who is this Mrs. Deneuve?" Cara asked Joseph. He knew everybody in the area.

"Some city woman," he said. "She must be loaded. She's practically rebuilt that old farmhouse."

Cara nodded. She knew the place well—she and Lucas often went past it on the way to Roly's Hill. She'd noticed construction workers there for weeks but had hardly given a thought to what that meant.

Feeling like her heart had finally broken, she crossed the paddock in search of Lucas. He trotted to her the instant he saw her, golden mane flowing.

"Hi, boy," she said. Lucas whinnied softly and searched her pockets for treats. The tears Cara had been holding back flooded down her face, spotting his thick winter coat. "Oh, how am I going to live without you?" she sobbed. Seeming to sense her misery, Lucas nuzzled her face. She flung her arms around his neck and buried her face in his silky mane. All she wanted to do was run away and avoid Mrs. Deneuve, but she couldn't—she had to see the whole awful business through all the way with Lucas.

The Deneuves arrived at two. By that time, Cara had managed to get a grip on herself. Mr. Roberts escorted a glamorous woman in her mid-thirties across the yard.

She looks like an old-fashioned movie star, Cara thought. Mrs. Deneuve had platinum blond hair and wore thick makeup. She was rather overdressed for a visit to a stable. Teetering on two-inch heels, she could hardly walk across the slippery yard. Behind her stomped two girls. One, about Cara's age, was pale and on the plump side. The other was about sixteen, dark and skinny with the same glitzy style as her mother. Both girls had in common a look of fury on their faces.

"What a magnificent place," said Mrs. Deneuve, gingerly sidestepping a puddle in the middle of the yard. "It's simply lovely. Isn't it, girls?"

The girls glared at her and grunted. Mrs. Deneuve, apparently used to their bad manners, ignored them and went on.

"I know they'll get to like the country," she told Mr. Roberts. "I just love it, myself. Country life is so healthy." To prove her point she took an enormous sniff of air, heavily laden with the scent of horse manure, and turned slightly green. "Now where is this *gorgeous* animal?" she asked hurriedly.

"Here he is," said Mr. Roberts, throwing open the stall door. "This is Cara," he said politely. "She's been looking after Lucas since my daughter went to Santa Barbara."

Mrs. Deneuve ignored Cara completely and stepped into the stall. The two girls glared at Cara like she was an alien. But a few seconds later their expressions were transformed by Lucas. They all stared at him as if they'd never seen a live horse before.

"He's, er . . . gorgeous," mumbled Mrs. Deneuve, nervously backing off toward the open door.

If the situation hadn't been so awful, Cara might have laughed. As it was she just stood there, puzzled by the scene. Not one of them responded naturally to

69

Lucas. Even when he turned his dark, trusting eyes on them, they continued to stare at him as if he were a slab of meat. When his questioning, gentle gaze met hers, she instinctively moved toward him and patted his neck. He lifted his head and blew softly into her hair, making the Deneuve family stampede in the direction of the stall door.

"He certainly is large," said Mrs. Deneuve, nearly slipping on the straw and falling on her glamorous bottom. "Isn't he impressive, girls?"

The girls didn't seem to think so. The older one looked disgusted, and the younger one looked scared to death. Cara's leaden heart ached. *Please, please, please don't buy him*, she kept saying to herself.

"Do you think he'll be suitable for my girls?" Mrs. Deneuve asked Mr. Roberts.

"Well, he's used to experienced riders and a lot of hard work," said Mr. Roberts. "But he's as gentle as a lamb. Patient, too, and very bright. He'd be good with beginners."

"That's all I need to hear," gushed Mrs. Deneuve, who obviously had more money than sense, Cara thought. "Let's discuss terms."

As they left the stable Mrs. Deneuve turned to Cara and addressed her for the first time. "Do you ride?" she asked.

Cara couldn't believe she was hearing right. Of course I ride! she felt like saying. Fortunately Mr. Roberts came to her rescue.

"She's an excellent rider. She could continue working Lucas," he added. "Just while your daughters are learning to ride."

"No, I don't think so," answered Mrs. Deneuve, a little too sharply.

"I can suggest a good local riding school," Mr. Roberts continued as they all followed him back across the yard.

"Marvelous!" cried Mrs. Deneuve, catching her high heels between the flagstones. "I'm sure the girls just can't wait."

The last sight Cara had of "the girls" was their scowling faces as they stomped off in their mother's wake.

A few minutes after they'd gone, Joseph hurried into the yard with a mischievous grin on his face. "What on earth is a family like that going to do with a horse?" he asked.

"Mrs. Deneuve hopes it will entertain her girls, I guess," answered Cara.

"She'll be lucky if they so much as go near him," Joseph said with a laugh. "Did you see the way they ran out of the stall? They were scared half to death!"

Cara hardly slept that night. Surely, *surely* Mr. Roberts wouldn't be so dumb as to sell Lucas to Mrs. Deneuve? What would they do with him, anyway? None of them could even ride!

Cara arrived at the stable the next morning and found Joseph waiting for her with a very worried expression.

"He's sold him!" Cara guessed immediately.

Joseph nodded grimly. He filled her in on the de-

71

tails. Because Mr. Roberts was fond of Lucas, he had arranged to visit him at the farmhouse from time to time. Mrs. Deneuve had met the asking price without argument, and she was rich enough to keep Lucas in some style and comfort. Mr. Roberts thought Lucas would have a good life, if not a challenging one.

"I have to drive him over to the farmhouse this afternoon," Joseph finished.

This afternoon! Cara felt the strength drain from her body. Her vision blurred, and suddenly she was falling down a spiraling black hole.

When she came to, she was lying on a hay bale in the tack room. Her head throbbed, and she felt sick.

"I've phoned your mom," said Joseph.

"No!" she cried, lifting herself up on one elbow. "I have to see Lucas."

"No, Cara," Joseph insisted, near tears himself. "It'll break your heart."

"My heart's already broken," she said, wiping the tears off her face. "Please, let me groom him this last time."

Joseph looked like he was going to say no.

"Please," she begged.

"Okay, if you say so," Joseph reluctantly agreed. "But I want you to call your mom. She's worried sick about you."

"I will," Cara said weakly. "Would you mind helping me up?" With Joseph supporting her, Cara struggled to her feet and tottered into the stable. The second she saw Lucas, she knew that he *knew*. Burying her face in his mane, she held on to him as if he were a lifeline.

"I'll leave you to it, missy," said Joseph tactfully.

She began grooming him, talking to him as if it were an ordinary day, but she couldn't keep up the pretense. Tears scalded her cheeks, and her voice broke as sobs wracked her body. Lucas nudged her affectionately, sniffing her hair and rubbing his head against her arm. Talking to him and being near him finally calmed Cara down a little. Suddenly she heard the dreaded scrunch of wheels outside in the yard and peered over the stable door. Joseph stood just outside.

"Now?" she asked.

"Afraid so," he said. His eyes looked watery.

Cara clipped a lead rope to Lucas's halter and handed it to Joseph. Lucas pulled back on the rope and looked around his stall for the last time. Then, perfect gentleman that he was, he calmly followed Joseph to the van and up the ramp.

"I'll come and see you, Lucas," Cara called, her voice breaking. "I love you!"

As Joseph slammed shut the gate of the van Lucas let out a loud whinny, as if to say, Good-bye!

"Good-bye, beautiful," Cara whispered over and over again. "Good-bye."

She waved until the van disappeared down the drive. Then she turned and walked back into Lucas's stall, which still smelled of him. Lying down in the warm straw, she put her head in her hands and wept uncontrollably. Late that night Mrs. Zol found her there, fast asleep in Lucas's empty stall.

9

THE ONLY WAY CARA SURVIVED THE NEXT FEW WEEKS WAS by doing everything automatically and not giving herself a moment to think. If she thought, she cried. Tansy was her staunch supporter through the long school hours. Her parents were wonderful too, but nothing took away the ache of her loss.

One day, just as she got home from school, the phone rang.

"Hello?" Cara said halfheartedly.

"I'm trying to teach those awful Deneuve girls how to ride," Ms. P. snapped with characteristic bluntness. "What a job!"

Cara's throat tightened. "How's Lucas?" she asked, her voice catching just at the mention of his name.

"He's fine—bored stiff, though. That's why I'm calling you."

Cara gripped the phone tightly.

"Mrs. Deneuve has a lot of crazy plans." Ms. P.

sighed wearily. "She has a boyfriend in Washington who's well connected with the local county set."

Cara knew who the county set were, although she wasn't one of them. Rich and sporty, they had showed up at every competitive event she'd been to with Ms. P. They were loud and boisterous, drank a lot of champagne in the refreshment tent, and seemed to enjoy each other's company far more than the sporting event itself. "Does her boyfriend ride?" Cara asked, puzzled.

"No, he plays *golf*," Ms. P. answered sharply.

Cara laughed at how disgusted she sounded. "Mrs. Deneuve can't stand golf either, so she's decided to make a local name for herself through horses," Ms. P. went on.

"But she can't even ride!" Cara cried.

"Exactly," said Ms. P. "But she's determined that one of her girls, preferably both girls, will ride Lucas."

Cara shook her head, mystified. Where was this conversation going?

"She has the ridiculous idea that Lucas will somehow be her introduction to the local county set." Ms. P. sniffed. "I've told her that if Lucas doesn't get worked good and hard this season, he'll be good for nothing at all. That frightened her. Then I suggested that you continue to school him and take him to the Culpeper show."

"Oh, Ms. P. You're just wonderful!" Cara cried impulsively.

"I wouldn't go quite that far," said Ms. P. "You and Lucas are a good team, and I'm backing you. So we're in business again. I'll see you Sunday, two o'clock sharp!" The phone clicked.

Cara slammed the receiver down and jumped three feet into the air. "*Whoopee!*" she yelled.

The Deneuves' old farmhouse was ten minutes farther down the road by bus from the Roberts place. It was a large estate, but not as old or as elegant as the Robertses'. The house's decor certainly wasn't as tasteful—the rambling red-brick house was stuffed full of chintz, chintz, and even more chintz.

Not that Cara was in the house for long. Mrs. Deneuve seemed eager to get her down to the stables, where she clearly thought Cara belonged. The stables were a little run-down and not nearly as smart as the Robertses' setup, but Cara didn't care. As long as she was with Lucas, nothing mattered.

"I can pay you a small amount," Mrs. Deneuve said as they walked around the stable yard. "Of course, once the girls have started jumping . . ."

Jumping! thought Cara. *They have to learn to ride first.*

". . . they'll do everything themselves."

Cara nodded politely. She would agree to anything to be near Lucas.

"It's just a question of them getting the knack," continued Mrs. Deneuve.

The knack? Cara couldn't believe she was hearing right. Mrs. Deneuve obviously thought that riding a horse was like changing a light bulb or fixing a broken bike.

76

"Ms. P. says you'll take good care of Lucas," said Mrs. Deneuve.

Cara nodded nervously.

"I'll expect a lot in return," said Mrs. Deneuve. "This horse business is expensive. I can't afford to have you lollygagging around."

Cara nodded vigorously. Anything, *anything* to be with Lucas.

"All right," finished Mrs. Deneuve. "I guess he's somewhere over there." She pointed vaguely toward a large paddock, then quickly tripped off in her ridiculous high heels.

Cara knew exactly where Lucas was. She could sense him before she saw him, like perfume on a breeze. She crept up and feasted her eyes on him, quietly grazing, his golden head bent, his silky mane gently lifting on the breeze.

"Hi, buddy," she whispered. Lucas's head shot up and he stared at her, as if he could hardly believe she was real.

"It's me," said Cara, half laughing, half crying. With a loud whinny the big chestnut threw back his head and trotted toward her.

"Oh, Lucas!" she cried, wrapping her arms around his muscled neck.

He nuzzled her, blew into her hair, and lipped her hands. Suddenly he smelled carrots, and started up their old game.

"Which hand?" she asked, holding out her closed fists. He sniffed first one, then the other, and lipped the one with the carrot.

"You're a genius!" she said, opening her hand. As he crunched the carrot, Cara whispered to him, "I'm back, boy. I'm going to look after you again. "

Lucas nuzzled her neck and face until she giggled. "It'll be just like old times, I promise you."

It turned out to be not at all like old times. Mrs. Deneuve treated Cara like a stable hand. She was expected to muck out the stall and put in fresh bedding, clean up the stable yard, hose down the aisles in the barn, polish the tack and—if there was half an hour left at the end of the day—ride Lucas. On top of everything, Mrs. Deneuve was a hard woman to please. If a wisp of straw blew around the yard, she'd grumble.

"You're treated worse than Cinderella," said Tansy, laughing.

The two girls were sitting outside the school, soaking up the early spring sunshine.

"Cinderella had it better than me," Cara answered. "But don't tell my parents."

"They really should know," said Tansy. "They'd be furious if they knew how badly she treats you."

"It's worth it," Cara said, smiling.

For all her complaining about expenses, Mrs. Deneuve didn't stint Lucas anything. She wanted him to look good and impress her new boyfriend and all her new friends in the county set. She made regular trips down to the stable yard to inspect his tack and admire him.

"You must be the best-fed and best-turned-out

horse in this county!" Cara said to Lucas as she mixed his feed one day. Lucas did look gorgeous. Cara felt that she herself was blooming from happiness.

"He's jumping better than ever," said Ms. P. after their Sunday lesson.

Cara smiled proudly. She felt they were working well together too. That awful time of separation had bonded them even closer, and everything they did together seemed especially wonderful.

Mrs. Deneuve never stopped reminding Cara of her girls' eagerness to ride, although Ms. P. told quite another story about their lessons with her.

"They don't do a thing," she said. "The older one always pretends to be sick, and the younger one tries, but she's scared to death. Sometimes I feel very sorry for Lucas."

Cara had been going to the old farmhouse for nearly two weeks before the Deneuve girls showed up in the yard. She had seen them around the house, but they'd never set foot near the stables. When they did, Cara really wished they hadn't. Their mother was dragging them along, forcing them every inch of the way. Cara could hear the older one arguing with her.

"I hate this place!" she cried. "I hate the country, and most of all I hate that horse!"

Cara stopped dead, shocked by the girl's uncontrolled anger.

"You'll like him soon," insisted Mrs. Deneuve.

"*No way!*" snarled the girl, white with fury.

"Then you're going to have to learn to, young

lady," snapped Mrs. Deneuve. "We're here to stay, whether you like it or not!" The girl burst into tears and ran toward the house.

"Come along, Sophie," commanded Mrs. Deneuve, grabbing the younger girl by the arm. "At least one of you can show some interest."

Sophie, obviously even more frightened of her mother than of Lucas, nervously crossed the yard. Cara was hosing down the concrete walk in front of the stalls.

"Can you turn that thing off?" said Mrs. Deneuve rudely.

Cara turned off the tap.

"This is Sophie," Mrs. Deneuve said, pushing her forward. "She wants to ride." Then, having issued her instructions, Mrs. Deneuve wobbled off in her high heels, leaving both girls staring at each other.

"I *don't* want to ride," Sophie whispered the moment her mother was out of earshot.

Cara nodded and smiled sympathetically. "I guessed," she said.

Sophie's face visibly relaxed. "That's good." She sighed. "But we'd better do something, just to keep Mom happy," she added anxiously.

"We'll clean the tack," said Cara. "Come on."

She took Sophie into the tack room, with its rows of sweet-smelling leather saddles and gleaming bits.

"This is nice," said Sophie, looking around with a pleased expression. "What should I do?"

"Shine up this bit," Cara said.

They worked together in awkward silence. Suddenly Sophie blurted, "You must think we're awful!"

Cara looked up, surprised. It was the first time any of the Deneuve family had spoken to her as if she was a person.

"No, I don't think you're awful," she answered truthfully. "I'm just confused by you all."

"*You're* confused," said Sophie with a hard laugh. "Try living with my mom. You'd be bouncing off the wall."

Cara didn't think it was her place to ask too many questions, but Sophie seemed anxious to talk to somebody.

"Do you like Virginia?" Sophie asked.

"Sure—it's my home," said Cara.

"But the countryside," Sophie went on. "Isn't it boring?"

Cara laughed. "No," she said. "It's beautiful." She saw Sophie's pale face crumple and added quickly, "You always like the place where you grew up, I guess."

"Sure! I love Washington," Sophie answered, suddenly aglow. "We still have the house there, but only Dad lives in it now." She paused. "My parents got divorced last year, and my mom bought this place and moved Vanessa and me out of public school to private school." She grimaced.

"I see," said Cara, busying herself with the bits. *No wonder the girls hate Virginia*, she thought. "It must be hard for you."

"It's awful!" Sophie cried. "First we leave Washington and Dad, then we get dumped in a new school, and now Mom thinks we're going to join the hicks and learn to ride. *I'm* not!" She stopped abruptly and blushed. "I'm sorry—I didn't mean you," she said.

"That's okay," Cara said, smiling reassuringly. "I'd be fed up too. Why did your mom think it would work to bring you guys out here in the first place?"

"Because of her new boyfriend in Washington. He kept raving about Virginia and the countryside and how good it would be for us." Sophie stopped for breath. "He's a real creep!" she added with a nasty smile.

Cara felt sorry for Sophie. What a mess. She didn't see how any of them could be happy.

"Vanessa and Mom fight all day long," Sophie said. "Sometimes I don't know what to do with myself."

"You should come down here," Cara suggested. "It's always quiet, and Lucas is a perfect gentleman. He'd never, ever upset you."

"I can see he's handsome," Sophie admitted. "I'm just so scared of horses."

"Take it slow with him," Cara advised. "But you can always hide out here. It'll keep your mom happy if she thinks you're riding," she added with a grin.

Sophie smiled back. Then her smile faded.

"You won't tell on me, will you?" she asked nervously.

"Never," Cara promised.

Almost every day after that Cara found Sophie in the tack room, reading a book or writing a letter and waiting for her. They dragged in hay bales to sit on. Sophie sneaked a jar of iced tea down from the house so that they could make drinks whenever they wanted, and Cara often brought homemade cake and cookies. Occasionally Lucas would pop his head over his stall door as they passed with their picnic, hoping for a cookie. Cara always played their game with him, closing her fists and making him guess before she gave him one. Sophie was delighted.

"Does he really know which hand the cookies are in?" she asked.

"Sure he does," said Cara. "Horses aren't dumb, you know."

"I always thought they were big and stupid," Sophie admitted. "And I didn't know they liked cookies."

"Well, now you know better."

As time went by and they began to trust each other more, Sophie told Cara how much she missed her dad.

"It's awful without him," she said one day, almost in tears. "We were always together when he wasn't working. Doing stuff like playing ball or going swimming. He's a lot of fun."

"When do you get to see him?" Cara asked.

"Once a month, if we're lucky. He travels around a lot, so sometimes it's every six weeks."

"Does your sister miss him as much as you do?" Cara asked.

"Van? I don't know," Sophie answered, sounding puzzled. "She hides her feelings about everything but her boyfriend. She's crazy about him."

"I've never seen her with a guy," Cara said.

"He's in D.C. That's why Van and Mom argue all the time—Van wants to go back, Mom wants to stay. She thinks country life is better for all of us."

"Where do you want to be?" Cara asked.

Sophie shrugged. "Me! I don't know. I just wish everybody would stop yelling at each other. At least I can get away from it down here," she said, smiling at Cara. Then her face clouded.

"We'd better watch out for Van," she said. "She keeps threatening me."

"Why?"

"She wants me to stop seeing you," Sophie said with a sigh.

"Really?" Cara said in surprise.

"She doesn't like you because you're a country girl. Even worse, you like horses and you're a great rider."

Cara frowned.

Sophie giggled and continued, "She's angry with me for making friends with you and liking Lucas." She glanced quickly behind them and whispered, "She's had this wild idea since we got here that if we give Mom a *really* hard time—refuse to ride or have anything to do with her creepy boyfriend—she'll pack up and move back to D.C."

"Your mom's not that stupid," Cara said.

"Yeah, I don't think so either," said Sophie. "I think Mom will stay in Virginia until she gets fed up with her boyfriend. She definitely won't move anywhere if we try to make her. But Van hates it here—she just wants to win." Sophie sighed heavily and took a huge bite of cookie. "She thinks you're

84

buttering up Mom so you can ride Lucas cheap."

"Oh, right," said Cara sarcastically.

"I know, it's stupid, but Van's not seeing anything straight lately," Sophie said.

The next day Cara found Sophie and Vanessa arguing in the stable yard.

"Don't lie to me about coming down here to ride!" Vanessa yelled at her sister. "I'm not as dumb as Mom. I know you're terrified of horses. All you do is hang around here and stuff yourself with cookies and talk to that stable girl."

"But I like it here!" Sophie cried, looking almost in tears. "And I like Cara, too."

Cara quickly ducked into the tack room.

"She's just using you!" Vanessa yelled. "She's got the best free ride in the county—do you really think she cares anything about you?" She approached Sophie menacingly. "I've told you *nothing* will stop me from going back to the city—nothing! Do you understand that?"

Sophie nodded rapidly.

"So stop playing around with horses and country girls, okay?" Vanessa stomped off to the house without waiting for an answer. Sophie burst into tears.

Cara came out of the tack room and quickly went over to Sophie.

"I'm sorry," she said, patting Sophie's trembling shoulder.

"Oh, it's all right," Sophie answered, digging in her jeans pocket for a tissue. "I'm used to it."

Cara wondered how anybody could get used to

being treated like that. "You shouldn't let her get away with it," she said angrily.

"I won't," Sophie said, suddenly straightening her shoulders. "I've decided I'm going to learn to ride Lucas, no matter what Van says!"

It was hard work even getting Sophie into the saddle. Cara talked her through it first to calm her down, explaining a hundred times exactly what they would do when she got on. Lucas behaved perfectly. He stood without moving a muscle while Sophie mounted.

"Lead me," Sophie begged. Her face was white.

"I'll stay right by you, I promise," Cara said patiently. She walked Sophie slowly around the ring. Sophie clutched the cantle of the saddle and slouched on Lucas like a bag of potatoes. But after about ten minutes she sat up a little straighter.

"Better?" Cara asked.

Sophie nodded, apparently unable to speak. They walked for about twenty minutes behind the stables, then Cara led them back to the yard.

Vanessa was waiting for them. Instantly the happy look on Sophie's face vanished.

"Do you really think you look good up there?" Vanessa sneered. "Well, you don't. You look fat and stupid."

Tears rushed into Sophie's eyes. She gripped Lucas's reins tightly.

"And *you*," Vanessa snarled, slowly walking toward Cara. "*You* stay out of this. We're going back to D.C. really soon, and if you or that horse gets in my way, you'll be sorry."

Vanessa lifted her fist. Lucas was startled and took

a quick step back, almost toppling Sophie.

"No!" cried Sophie.

"See what I mean?" shouted Vanessa. "That's a dangerous animal!"

"He is not," Cara said angrily. "Why don't you learn how to treat him properly?"

"He's *my* horse and I'll treat him any way I please," Vanessa snapped. "Just remember that, or you'll be out of a job." Turning on her heel, she stormed out of the yard.

"Come on, I'll help you down," Cara said to Sophie, pulling her right foot out of the stirrup. Lucas stood patiently while Sophie slithered down.

"Thanks, Lucas," Sophie said, holding out a carrot. Lucas very gently took the carrot from her hand and solemnly crunched it. When he'd finished, he nudged her arm for more. Sophie burst out laughing. "He really is cute," she said.

"You did fine," Cara said, smiling.

"Until my sister showed up," Sophie said grimly.

"She's got real problems." Cara unbuckled Lucas's saddle and carried it to the tack room.

"I'm scared of her," Sophie admitted, following her. "I think she'll go crazy if Mom keeps her locked away in the country much longer."

"Can't she go visit her boyfriend?" Cara asked hopefully. "That might calm her down a little."

Sophie shook her head. "We aren't going to D.C. till Easter."

Easter, thought Cara. *Another month of Vanessa like this. I don't even want to think about what she'll do next.*

10

WITH ONLY THREE WEEKS LEFT BEFORE THE CULPEPER show, Cara was frantically busy. She was working flat-out at school, preparing for tests in several subjects, and flat-out with Lucas, preparing for the regional finals. Ms. P. worked her till she nearly dropped, but it had its effect. Four-foot jumps suddenly didn't seem so awesome anymore.

"They'll never be a breeze, though," she said to Ms. P.

"Just wait till we reach five foot," said Ms. P.

Cara swallowed. She doubted Ms. P. was joking—she never joked when it came to horses.

There weren't enough hours each day for everything Cara had to do, and time seemed to speed up as the show approached. The constant pressure she was under began to take its toll. She grew pale and lost weight, and she had dark circles under her eyes. Her parents watched her with obvious concern, but resisted nagging her about how tired she looked. Her dad did say that once the show was over, she had to put school first and start taking care of herself.

Cara quickly agreed. She would consent to anything as long as nobody got in her way between now and March 21.

Then her workload increased—Ms. P. threw in a couple of extra lessons free.

"But I owe you so much already!" Cara protested.

"Nonsense!" said Ms. P. dismissively. "You can always pay me back when you're rich and famous."

I don't think that will be for a while, Cara thought. But she gratefully accepted the extra lessons.

During the week before the show, she and Lucas performed so superbly that even their instructor was impressed.

"He adores jumping," Ms. P said delightedly. "You're a perfect team. If you keep this up for just for one more week, you'll walk away with that trophy."

Cara felt her stomach flutter. She and Lucas were so psyched for the event, she almost wished it were right now, not days away.

"I hope I haven't peaked too soon," she said to Sophie, who had been watching their lesson.

"I don't know how you do it!" Sophie gasped, wide-eyed. "You just *soar*. I swear you and Lucas could fly if you wanted."

"Sometimes it feels like that," Cara said dreamily. "When I give him his head at a jump, it's like an explosion going off underneath me. I love it!"

"I can see that," said Sophie. "You sometimes

laugh out loud when you clear the jumps. I envy you." She sighed.

"Why?" Cara asked. "You're doing well yourself."

Sophie flushed with pleasure. Over the past week she'd progressed from being led by Cara to walking Lucas on her own, for five minutes to start with, then ten, and finally to half an hour a day.

"I'm beginning to trust Lucas," she said shyly.

"Good," said Cara. "He likes you too."

Unfortunately Vanessa had been on the warpath all week, and Sophie's success just seemed to be making her worse. Sophie and Cara were stirring up iced tea in the tack room when Vanessa burst in on them.

"I'm riding!" she announced.

Cara stared at her in horror. With less than a week to the show, the last thing Lucas needed was a bad-tempered novice on his back.

"Well, tack him up!" commanded Vanessa.

"Okay," Cara said, trying to think what to do. "Would you like me to lead you, just until you get used to him?"

Vanessa stared at Cara as if she was something that had crawled out of the woodwork.

"No," she sneered. "I've had lessons from a professional. I can do without *you!*"

With a premonition of disaster, Cara tacked up Lucas, fumbling with the bridle and saddle. Catching her nervousness, Lucas pawed the ground impatiently.

"I'm sorry, buddy," she whispered into his mane. "I know you just had a lesson, but we have to do what your owner wants." He was still hot, so she wiped down his chest and legs.

"Hurry up!" bawled Vanessa. "I don't have all day."

"He's tired, Van," Sophie said timidly. "He just finished a jumping lesson."

"Tired!" scoffed her sister. "He's done nothing for weeks. It's about time he earned his keep." She pitched her voice higher. "He isn't here exclusively for stable girls to ride, you know."

"Van, are you sure you can ride him?" Sophie asked, her voice wobbling.

"Well, I won't be walking him around the ring like you!" Vanessa snapped.

Cara led Lucas into the yard, her heart pounding. Lucas stood quietly as always, waiting for Vanessa to mount.

Vanessa grabbed the reins and jammed her boot into one of the stirrups. Winded by the blow, Lucas moved slightly to one side. Vanessa slid back to the ground.

"This horse has no manners!" she shrieked, making everybody jump, Lucas included.

"He has perfect manners," said Cara, trying to keep her self-control. "He was just startled when you kicked him. Why don't I give you a leg up?" she asked, cupping her hands.

"No!" Vanessa snapped. "I can do it myself." Again she threw herself at Lucas and heaved herself up, kicking him like he was a brick wall. Finally she scrambled into the saddle. Whacking him with her boots and holding the reins way too high, she set off out of the yard at a brisk, ungainly trot.

"Oh, God," Sophie whispered the moment Vanessa couldn't hear her. "She can't ride at all!"

Cara was trying hard not to panic. *I've got to keep them in sight*, she thought. "Where's your bike?" she asked Sophie.

"In the garage."

"Get it and follow Van, but not too close," Cara ordered. "I'll run through the woods and watch them."

Cara ran as fast as she could along the edge of the wood that bordered one side of the farm and managed to catch up with them. Halfway down the drive Vanessa's trot had quickened, and she was bouncing all over the place. Her legs were waving around as she tried unsuccessfully to get a grip on Lucas, who she kept yelling at.

Cara had a long view of the drive from where she was running. To her horror, she saw Mrs. Deneuve's car sweep into the drive. *Time to put a stop to this ride*, she thought, and burst onto the drive, waving her arms.

Vanessa looked up and saw both Cara and the car. She scowled, then suddenly kicked Lucas into a canter. Her bouncing and flopping intensified. Screaming hysterically, she dropped the reins and flung herself forward onto his neck.

"*Lucas!*" Cara cried. Hearing her voice, he stopped immediately. Vanessa slithered over his neck and landed in a heap on the drive just as Mrs. Deneuve swooped around the corner. Slamming on the brakes, she jumped out of the car and ran to where Vanessa was lying on the ground.

Cara got there first. Vanessa's eyes were open, but by the time her mother was beside her, they were shut.

"Oh, no!" gasped Mrs. Deneuve. "She's unconscious."

Cara wanted to point out that Vanessa's eyelashes were fluttering and her cheeks were a healthy pink. But she only said, "I think she's okay."

Sophie skidded to a stop beside them on her bike. "Go home and call the doctor!" her mother screamed.

Sophie, who was red and sweaty and really looked like she might faint, obediently turned the bike around and set off for the house.

"Help me lift her," Mrs. Deneuve snapped at Cara. Between them they carried Vanessa to the car and gently lowered her onto the backseat.

"I'll speak to you later," growled Mrs. Deneuve, slamming the car door and roaring off.

Throughout the drama Lucas had stayed quiet and still, a puzzled look in his dark eyes.

"It's okay, boy," Cara said, gently running her hand over his sweaty flanks. "You didn't do anything wrong. But that awful Vanessa has gotten us in trouble again." She glumly led him back down the drive to the peace and quiet of his stall.

As she was brushing him Sophie appeared.

"Things are crazy in the house," she whispered.

Cara was shocked to see that she was shaking all over. "Let's go sit in the tack room," she said. Sophie sank onto a bale of hay, put her head in her hands, and sobbed.

"Don't worry about Vanessa," Cara said. "She's all

93

right. I saw her before your mother did, and she was fine. She's just faking it."

"I know that and the doctor knows that," Sophie said through her tears. "The only person dumb enough not to know it is Mom! She's flipping out."

"Isn't that just what Vanessa wants?" Cara asked slowly. "Now she's got your mom on her side at last."

"Yeah," Sophie agreed. "Not a bad plan, really."

If you don't mind almost breaking your neck to make the point, Cara thought irritably.

"Is Lucas okay?" Sophie asked.

Cara nodded. "I checked him out—he's just hot and tired. He's had an awful afternoon, poor guy. I'd better go put on his blanket and fix him a bran mash."

Sophie went to the feed room with her, then stayed by Lucas, fussing over him. The day's events seemed to have made her less afraid of him.

Cara and Sophie were so absorbed in taking care of Lucas that neither of them heard the familiar *click-click* of Mrs. Deneuve's heels on the stones in the yard.

"Well, I'm glad to see you're keeping an eye on at least *one* of my daughters," she snapped over the stall door. Sophie jumped a mile. Cara braced herself for a thorough dressing down.

"I hold you responsible for this incident," said Mrs. Deneuve, glaring at her. "Vanessa should not have been allowed out of this yard unsupervised."

Cara opened her mouth to speak, but Sophie got there first.

"Mom, that's just not fair," she said. "Vanessa

stormed in here and wouldn't let Cara lead her. I saw—"

"Shut up!" her mother said icily. "Get in the house this minute."

Sophie slunk out, her head drooping.

"If you don't do your job better than this, you won't have one," Mrs. Deneuve warned. "Another accident like this one, and you're out."

Cara waited until she had gone, then pressed her forehead into Lucas's soft mane and groaned. "Oh, Lucas, can't they just leave us alone until Saturday?"

Fortunately school kept everybody busy, for most of the week at least. Neither Vanessa nor Mrs. Deneuve visited the stable once. Sophie came when she could. Cara liked Sophie more and more, and Lucas did too. He would pop his head over the stall door when he saw her and whinny, nudging her for treats when she got close, just as he did with Cara. Sophie copied Cara's game with him, holding out her closed fists and asking him to choose which hand held the carrot. When he lipped the hand with the carrot, she would laugh delightedly.

"I never thought I could feel like this about a horse," she admitted to Cara.

"Everybody falls in love with Lucas," said Cara proudly. "It's just a question of how long it takes."

"I don't think that applies to Van, somehow," said Sophie with a grin.

"I think your sister will probably prove an exception to the rule," Cara agreed.

Sophie declined a riding lesson that week.

95

"I don't want to make things worse for you," she said. "Mom's calmed down now that Van's out of bed and getting 'well.'" She shook her head. "Boy, did she get a lot of mileage out of that fall."

"If only your mom would let her visit her boy-friend this weekend," said Cara wistfully. "It would be nice to know that she was out of the way in Washington."

"Not a chance," Sophie said. "Vanessa's coming to the show to keep Mom company, she says. I think she just wants to make more trouble for you and Lucas."

Cara felt her stomach lurch. "Do you really think she's planning something?" she asked.

"From the creepy way she's behaving, I'd say yes," said Sophie. "It's scary—she and Mom have been friendly all week. Talking about what they'll wear, and dumb things like that. It's fishy."

"Fishy?" Cara repeated thoughtfully. "It stinks."

Every night she had terrible dreams about Vanessa. One night she dreamed Vanessa cut the girth on Lucas's saddle, another night that Vanessa threw red paint on her riding outfit. On the night before the show she woke up drenched with sweat after dreaming that Vanessa had slashed the tires on the horse van.

"You look terrible," said Mrs. Zol every morning.

I feel terrible, Cara thought, but now wasn't the time to tell her mother the truth. At school she confided in Tansy.

"Sometimes I think Vanessa's a witch!" Cara whispered during math class.

"She's just a dumb girl who can't ride. What else can she do?" Tansy whispered back.

"A lot," Cara said worriedly. "I don't care what she does to me. It's Lucas I'm worried about."

"She wouldn't dare hurt a valuable horse like him, would she?" Tansy looked shocked.

"I don't know," said Cara wearily, just before the math teacher shushed them.

Ms. P. gave her a final lesson on the Friday afternoon before the show. She'd set up a tight course of four-foot jumps and paid particular attention to Cara's approach and her use of the space between the jumps. When she was nervous, Cara had a tendency to fiddle with Lucas's mouth near the fences, a habit he hated.

"You'll unbalance him!" Ms. P. called out. "Find his stride and make your adjustments ahead of the fence. Keep your eye on the fence!" she yelled as Cara took a corner. "Don't look down, look ahead!"

Cara quickly responded to Ms. P.'s instructions, looking forward, encouraging Lucas to anticipate what was coming next. "Easy now," she whispered as she took a corner and lined him up. The last thing she wanted was to come at the fence from an angle. She pressed him on with her legs, then checked him in and zipped straight over the middle of the bright red pole.

"Perfect!" Ms. P. cried delightedly. Cara smiled with pleasure and repeated the corner jumps until she and Lucas were perfectly synchronized. After about a quarter of an hour Ms. P. called, "Okay, finish now, while he's on a high. You don't want him getting bored."

Cara trotted Lucas back to the stable yard, where Ms. P. joined her.

"You've both worked well," she said, patting Lucas's sweating neck. "Just remember to anticipate turns, Cara. You can drop vital speed points if you don't concentrate and he loses the right stride."

Cara nodded. That was basic stuff, but with show nerves creeping up on her, she needed reminding. "I know," she said apologetically.

"You have a natural eye for positioning yourself. Fix your attention on the course ahead—it'll keep Lucas on his toes if he's always anticipating you. And keep that leg on him. If he knows you're encouraging him, physically and mentally, he'll fly through the course." Seeing Cara's worried expression, Ms. P. said, "There's something on your mind. I want to know what it is."

Cara shuffled awkwardly. "I'm . . . nervous," she admitted.

"Nervous?" Ms. P. repeated, and waited.

"It's that family," Cara blurted, nodding toward the farmhouse. "They're so screwed up, they're dangerous."

Ms. P. frowned. "They are extremely strange," she said. "But what does that have to do with riding Lucas in the Culpeper show?"

Cara hadn't told Ms. P. about Vanessa's "accident" before, but suddenly it all came out. Ms. P. listened tight-lipped until Cara had finished.

"Stupid girl!" she cried. "She could have seriously injured that horse. I'll speak to her mother about this."

"No, please don't!" Cara cried. "That would make Vanessa even meaner. She might really hurt Lucas next time."

Ms. P.'s eyebrows shot up in alarm. "What else do you think she has in mind?" she asked.

Cara shook her head. "I don't know. She'll be at the show on Saturday, and I'm sure it's not to watch—she wants to ruin things for me and Lucas. I can feel it."

"We'll just have to make sure she doesn't, won't we?" Ms. P. said icily.

Cara felt better. If Ms. P. helped her, she felt sure she would be able to conquer jumps, Vanessa, or anything else.

But that night, just as she was leaving the stable, Cara saw Vanessa slip out of the tack room. Cara jumped with fright.

"Don't try too hard tomorrow," Vanessa said harshly.

Cara said nothing. Whatever she said would just antagonize Vanessa more.

"By the way, I burned your leg wraps," Vanessa added viciously.

Cara still said nothing, but after Vanessa had gone, she swore under her breath. She had to wrap Lucas's legs for the van trip or he might hurt them badly.

"Joseph!" she said suddenly out loud, and ran

down the road to the Robertses' farm. Joseph was delighted to see her and readily agreed to lend her Stephanie's old wraps.

"Nobody needs them around here these days," he said sadly. "I sure do miss that horse. How is he?"

"He's perfect," Cara answered. "It's the family that's awful."

Joseph nodded. "You could see trouble coming the minute Mrs. Deneuve walked into this stable." His mischievous smile wrinkled his tanned face. "She doesn't know the tail from the head of a horse!"

Cara burst out laughing. It felt good to talk to Joseph again. She looked longingly around the stable yard and stared wistfully into Lucas's old stall.

"I miss you," she murmured.

"I miss you too," Joseph admitted. "And that old horse neighing at me every morning for his breakfast."

"I'll bring him over for a visit," Cara promised. "Just as soon as the Culpeper show is over."

"With all your blue ribbons," Joseph added. "Good luck, missy. I'll be thinking about you tomorrow."

Cara ran for her bus home. As she sat back in her seat and watched the countryside flash by the window she went through her plans for the next day. Everything was all set. She was ready, Lucas was ready—the only thing that could stop them was Vanessa. What was she planning?

11

CARA ARRIVED AT THE STABLES JUST AFTER DAWN, ANXIOUS to finish her preparations before Mrs. Deneuve turned up and started nagging her. Sophie walked into the stable just before nine, while Cara was waiting for the van.

"Wow! You look fantastic," she said, admiring Cara's well-tailored show-jumping outfit.

"The only problem is it's hard to keep clean." Cara picked specks of hay from her immaculate cream jodhpurs.

"Wait till you see Mom," Sophie said, giggling.

"I'm glad she's not here to help," said Cara sourly.

"She's too busy with her wardrobe to be bothered with anybody," Sophie answered. "She bought jodhpurs, riding boots, *and* a yellow slicker! She looks like a country squire. Except her boots are killing her, and she's limping."

Cara smiled at the thought of Mrs. Deneuve replacing her pointy high heels with riding boots.

"What about Vanessa?" she asked. "Is she acting any better?"

"Nope—the same," said Sophie. Her face suddenly fell.

"Now what?" Cara said. Her heart began to beat faster.

"Poor Van." Sophie sighed. "She came to my room last night. She acted scared to death and cried a lot. I think she's losing it."

She lost it a long time ago, Cara thought.

"I know she's been mean most of the time she's been here, but she's my sister, and I promise you, she hasn't always been this crazy." Sophie looked at Cara as if she wanted very much for Cara to believe her.

"Sophie, it's really hard for me to feel sorry for Vanessa," Cara said. "I'm sure what you're saying is true, but right now, she's dangerous and I'm afraid of her."

"I'm really scared of her too," Sophie said. "Especially after what she said last night."

"What?" Cara asked quickly.

"She said she's so miserable, she'll do *anything* to get Mom to move back to D.C. She just wants to be with Dad and her boyfriend again."

"Why didn't she say all that to your mother?" Cara asked impatiently. "I mean, I guess it's reasonable that she wants to go back."

"Because Mom won't listen!" Sophie said angrily. "Since she and Dad split up, all she thinks about is living in the country and getting to know all Gary's rich friends."

"Who's Gary?" Cara asked.

"Her creepy boyfriend from D.C.," said Sophie.

Cara shrugged. She didn't need to hear all this family history just before the show.

Sophie said hurriedly, "All I'm saying is that as long as Mom won't listen to what Van says, she won't stop trying to get at you, me, and Lucas. It's the only way she can make Mom pay attention to her."

Great, Cara thought. *Just great.*

Mrs. Deneuve was waving at Sophie from the drive. "I'd better go," Sophie said. "I'll see you there. If I don't catch you before your first class, good luck!"

Cara watched the Deneuves' car zoom down the drive, her mind feverishly turning over the possibilities of what Vanessa might do next. Although it was okay for Sophie to feel sorry for her sister—Cara supposed somebody had to—she herself couldn't waste time on it. She couldn't sit around and wait for the next disaster to happen.

Cara stood in the stable yard for about fifteen minutes, watching for the van. "Where is it?" she said out loud. Suddenly panicking, she ran up to the farmhouse and knocked on the front door. The housekeeper, a local woman who knew Cara well, let her in.

"Hi, there," she said cheerfully. "I thought you would have been on your way by now, dear."

"Me too," said Cara. "The van hasn't come. Do you know the name of the driver Mrs. Deneuve hired?"

103

The housekeeper shook her head. "Maybe she left the number over there." She nodded at a notepad lying by the telephone. Cara grabbed it and flicked through it.

"Van rental," she muttered. "Here it is!" She quickly dialed the number. A few seconds later a man answered, "Hello."

Cara gasped with relief. "Oh, hello, it's Cara Zol," she said breathlessly. "I just wondered, where are you?"

"Right here at home," he answered.

"Why aren't you here?"

"Somebody phoned last night and canceled the van," he explained.

"Canceled!" Cara gasped. "Who canceled it?"

"A girl," said the man. "I didn't catch her name."

Vanessa! Cara thought angrily. Fighting to keep her voice calm, she said, "Can you come right away?"

"Sure, I'll be there in ten minutes."

Cara put down the phone and glanced at her watch. It was nearly nine thirty. It took two hours to get to Culpeper, and her first class was scheduled for twelve. She might just make it.

Yelling good-bye to the housekeeper, she ran down the path back to the stable. There she leaned against the door to the feed room and fought for self-control. Whatever happened, she couldn't let all this get to her. That would mean Vanessa had won.

She took several long, deep breaths, then walked up to Lucas's stall.

"Sorry, boy," she said, tickling his ears. "We have a slight technical hitch."

104

When the van drove up, Cara loaded Lucas in record time, then jumped into the passenger seat and they were off.

"Thank goodness," she said with a sigh, sinking back into her seat. The trip couldn't have been more different from the one she and Joseph had made to the Barracks show just a few months earlier. Cara sat silently staring out the window, her mind again frantically going through all the disasters Vanessa might have cooked up for her. So far, she'd burned the leg wraps and canceled the van. What lay in wait for her at Culpeper?

Then Cara had a comforting thought. Vanessa must be assuming that Cara wasn't going to make it to the show. In that case, she wouldn't have plotted anything more. Cara settled back into her seat with relief. *Maybe things will work out after all*, she thought. Especially if the show was running late, which often happened.

Luckily the highways were clear, and they made good time. They drove through Culpeper around eleven thirty and into the packed showgrounds at about eleven forty-five. The grounds were chockful of horse vans, making parking difficult.

"I'll catch up with you later," Cara said to the driver, jumping out of the van at the show office. "I just want to see if they're running late."

Luckily all the classes were fifteen minutes behind schedule. *Perfect*, Cara thought as she headed back to the van. *I'll have just enough time to get Lucas ready and let him stretch his legs before the Open Jumping class starts.*

As she dropped the ramp for him Lucas whinnied loudly.

"You old show-off," Cara said fondly. Lucas pranced out, tossing his head. Cara grabbed his halter. "Come on, let's work off some of that energy before you hurt yourself."

She quickly tacked him up and mounted, then set off at a brisk trot out of the showgrounds and across some open fields. There she gave him his head and let him gallop. After the exercise she felt much calmer, and Lucas had settled down too. When they got back to the show ring, Ms. P. was waiting for them.

"Where on earth have you been?" she snapped.

"I'll explain later," said Cara, not wanting to get drawn into a horrible scene three minutes before the starting bell rang.

"Vicki's in the ring now," said Ms. P. "Doing well, I think."

As if to prove her right, there was a burst of applause and Vicki cantered out, her eyes shining.

"Clear round for Vicki Wolfe on Merlin's Wand," boomed the commentator's voice over the loud-speaker.

"Good luck!" Vicki called as the girls passed in the ring.

"Number thirty-three, Erin's Luck, ridden by Cara Zol, owned by Mrs. Lucille Deneuve."

A flutter of excitement among the spectators made Cara glance to her left. There she saw Mrs. Deneuve preening herself, Vanessa scowling, and Sophie smiling and giving her a thumbs-up.

106

Cara turned her attention to the course, which she hadn't even had a chance to walk. She was stunned, not by the height of the jumps—she had expected four feet—but by the tight turns and difficult combinations. The course began with a big cross jump, followed by some plank jumps and a combination: a tricky double with a short stride between the fences. A very tight turn at a big blue-and-white wall worried Cara even from a distance. More combinations followed—a triple, a combination of three separate gates with a stride between each, and another double—and the course finished with a wide water jump. The layout of the jumps itself wasn't remarkable; what daunted Cara was the short distances between all the fences.

We'd better make tight turns, she thought. Then she saw Ms. P. watching her and smiled. Tight turns were exactly what she and Lucas had practiced in their last lesson: trust her experienced instructor to have anticipated such a course.

A surge of confidence rushed through Cara. Sensing it, Lucas's ears pricked expectantly. At last she and Lucas were here, Cara thought, doing what they did best together, and Vanessa couldn't spoil it for them now.

"Go for it, buddy!" she cried, and Lucas took the first fence as if he had wings. Both of them were overexcited after he almost danced over the plank jumps, and he came up too fast on the first combination. Lucas popped the jump and they made it over clean, but Cara had given him his head for too long and let him build up too much speed. She couldn't pull him up fast enough after he'd cleared the poles to collect him for the next jump.

The huge blue-and-white wall bore down on them. Checking Lucas as much as she could, Cara tried to give him time to balance himself and find his stride. She felt him shift his weight, ready for takeoff, and they shot over, apparently in a perfect glide.

Yes! she thought. Or had Lucas just ticked the top layer of bricks? Glancing behind her, she saw the top blue bricks wobble. Then she heard a horrible crash as the entire wall collapsed onto the ground behind them.

"Oh, no!" Cara cried. She could feel sweat breaking out on her forehead. Lucas cantered easily on, apparently unruffled.

Get ahold of yourself, she thought as they approached the triple gate and massive double combination. Lucas kept his rhythm and arched beautifully over both jumps, then sailed over the water jump. That meant they had completed the course with only four faults.

After the way this morning started out, it's amazing I didn't knock down every jump in sight, Cara thought.

Ms. P. didn't seem too upset by the flawed performance. "You got control again nicely," she said, "and your round was sufficient to advance you to the finals this afternoon. Well done."

Sophie was waiting outside in the warm-up ring.

"Oh, Cara, you were wonderful!" she cried, her face glowing. "So were you, Lucas. You clever boy."

108

Patting Lucas the whole way, Sophie walked with them back to the parking lot and the van.

After they'd untacked Lucas, Cara suddenly realized she was starving. "Would you stay with Lucas while I run down to the refreshment tent to grab something to eat?" she asked Sophie.

"Sure," Sophie said, beaming. "I'll take really good care of him."

"Thanks," said Cara. It was a relief to be able to trust somebody with Lucas.

"Don't worry." Sophie tightened her grip on Lucas's lead rope. "Take as long as you like. I'll pat him and talk to him so he stays calm."

As long as you don't let Vanessa near him, he'll be fine, Cara thought. She didn't say anything to Sophie, though—she was scared enough of her sister.

In the refreshment tent Cara walked straight into Mrs. Deneuve. Lucas's owner was flushed with excitement and waving a goblet of champagne.

"My dear!" she called. "You gave me such a fright. I really thought you were going to miss your first class."

Cara noticed Vanessa watching her, eyes narrowed like a cat's. Cara smiled and shrugged. "I'm sorry you were worried. We just had a little trouble loading Lucas, that's all." She felt awful lying about Lucas, who was a perfect angel to load, but she had no intention of letting Vanessa get any satisfaction out of her mean trick.

Cara quickly bought a sandwich and soft drink and politely excused herself. Just as she was leaving, Mrs. Deneuve whispered, "Bring Lucas into the warm-up ring early. I want to show him off to my friends."

She sauntered off, obviously very pleased with herself. Cara walked slowly back to the van, deep in thought. Mrs. Deneuve paid the bills, and so if she wanted Lucas in the ring early, then she got him there. But one thing was certain: although a long wait before the class might suit her, it wouldn't do Lucas any good—he would get bored and restless.

"Are you all right?" asked Ms. P., catching Cara as she crossed the parking lot.

"No," said Cara, suddenly unable to bottle up her anxieties any longer. "That terrible Vanessa is trying to sabotage my every move—she even canceled the van this morning—and now her mother wants to show Lucas off to all her friends *before* the final."

Ms. P. smacked her whip hard against her boot. "Stupid woman!" She turned on her heel. "I'll talk to her immediately!"

Cara watched her go, feeling a mixture of relief that something was being done about the situation and fear that things would just get worse.

Ten minutes later Ms. P. strode up to Cara, who was sitting with Sophie on the grass beside the van. "Mrs. Deneuve thinks it's best not to have Lucas hanging around too long before the final," she said, winking. "Bring him into the ring just before four. I'll see you then—I have to attend to a student in the next class."

"Wow!" said Sophie when Ms. P. was out of earshot. "She must be the only person in the world my mom listens to!"

After the long lunch break, three events would take place before the finals. Cara didn't want to tack Lucas up and have him hanging around for hours, so she tied him to the side of the van, strung a hay net, and left him in peace. She and Sophie sat on the grass beside him, enjoying the spectacle of the show all around them.

Finally at about three o'clock Cara stood up and stretched. "Time for action," she said.

Sophie left them alone to prepare themselves for the big event. Cara talked to Lucas as she slipped on his bridle and fastened the straps.

"We're going to have a blast!" she said. Lucas nudged her affectionately, his eyes bright. "But you've got to be good and not run away with yourself," Cara continued as she put the saddle on his back and fastened the girth. "Breathe in," she said, pulling the buckles tighter by a notch.

When they were both ready, Cara mounted up and walked Lucas around for a while, letting him get used to the surroundings again. As usual, Lucas enjoyed showing off to the other horses. Tossing his mane and picking up his feet as he trotted by the other competitors, he seemed very pleased with himself.

"Let's get down to business," Cara said. She trotted and cantered him around the warm-up ring until she felt his body relax and become supple under her. Then she tried him out on the practice fences. He went over every one like a dream.

Anxious not to bore Lucas with too much practice work, yet wanting to keep him lively and expectant

111

for the event, Cara took him out of the showgrounds to the fields behind them. There she gave him his head, and they had a fast, spirited gallop. As she eased him back into a canter, Lucas snorted and did a little spring into the air, obviously enjoying the outing.

Cara didn't rush him back but walked him slowly along the hedges, giving him time to cool off and herself a chance to enjoy the robins' song and the soft green lushness of the warm spring day. Lucas sniffed the air around him, stopping occasionally to watch a bee or a bird. Finally he seemed to make up his mind that it was time to be serious. With a last toss of his head he trotted toward the showgrounds.

"You are such a professional," Cara whispered. "I just hope I live up to your performance."

A crowd was gathering around the newly laid-out course. Leaving Lucas in Ms. P.'s competent hands, Cara and Vicki walked it, carefully measuring out the turns and variations in distance. The strides between the triple combination were tight, and a careful approach to the first fence would be critical to avoid knocking down all three fences. Although it was the largest course Cara had ever jumped, it was wide and clear, and she was pretty sure she'd have enough time between jumps to collect Lucas and get him well balanced for the next fence.

"How are you feeling?" Vicki asked.

"Like Jell-O," Cara confessed. "Lucas is the hero. He's bombproof—I'm not!"

As if to prove her point, she found Lucas patiently waiting with Ms. P., watching the other horses and apparently having a pleasant time. But Vicki's horse, Merlin, was working himself into a state. His fine Arab breeding had given him a fiery, temperamental nature, and he hated the fuss and noise of crowds. The mounting tension of the spectators was increasingly getting on his nerves.

Cara admired Merlin tremendously—both his fine lines and beautiful jumping style, in which he always soared like a bird and landed so lightly he barely raised dust. But she suspected Vicki had serious problems ahead today. It wouldn't be easy to calm him down at this stage.

"Good luck," she said as Vicki trotted Merlin away from the crowd. But a few minutes later it was Cara who needed the luck. Mrs. Deneuve glided up with a group of friends, who flocked around Lucas.

"Isn't he a dear!" exclaimed Mrs. Deneuve.

"Wonderful."

"So strong."

"Magnificent."

Suddenly Cara heard Vanessa's voice snap through the murmurs of admiration. "Of course I should be riding him myself," she said, pushing her way through to the front. "Unfortunately I had a bad fall last week, so we had to get one of the stable hands in to ride him. She's not worth much."

All eyes turned to Cara, who blushed crimson. Suddenly a middle-aged man with piercing blue eyes and a warm smile said, "She did very well in the first round."

There was a collective mutter of agreement.

"Yes, of course," said Mrs. Deneuve, briskly covering up her daughter's rudeness. "Now, Cara, shall I hold Lucas while you put on your coat?"

The last thing Cara wanted was to leave Lucas alone near Vanessa Deneuve.

"No," she answered sharply. "I mean, no, thank you, not right now. I'll ride him around a little more and put on my coat later," she quickly added. "Thank you anyway."

Mrs. Deneuve gave her a regal nod and sailed off like she was the queen of England. Cara groaned. Leaning down from the saddle, she whispered into Lucas's pricked ears, "This is *really* tough for me."

Lucas huffed excitedly, eager to get to work. Cara took him over the practice jumps one last time. Then she spotted Sophie waiting for her just outside the ring, ghostly pale even from a distance. They'd arranged to meet just before the competition started. Why had she turned up early?

Cara cantered up to the fence. "What's wrong?" she asked.

Sophie's eyes were brimming with tears. Wordlessly she held up Cara's new riding coat, which had been slashed from top to bottom.

"No!" gasped Cara. "No, this can't have happened!"

"I didn't leave the van for a second, I swear I didn't!" cried Sophie, tears streaming down her plump cheeks. "The only person who came near was Vanessa—" She stopped short, her jaw dropping. "Oh, Cara, I'm so sorry."

114

"Vanessa!" Cara said through clenched teeth.

"What are we going to do?" sobbed Sophie, almost hysterical.

"Think fast," said Cara, suddenly icy calm. She had no intention of being beaten by Vanessa now, after she and Lucas had suffered so much from her and come so far in spite of it. She and Lucas had already proved twice that they could triumph over her scheming plots. They were going to *win* this show!

"The first contestant in today's regional finals," boomed the announcer over the loudspeaker system, "is number seventeen, Sonia Brynstein on Lady Luck."

"Cara!" yelled Sophie. "You're running out of time!"

At that moment Ms. P. walked into the ring. "Shouldn't you be putting him over a few jumps?" she inquired briskly.

"Yes," said Cara, and held up the shredded coat.

"More sabotage?" asked Ms. P. calmly.

Cara nodded. To her astonishment, Ms. P. whipped off her own immaculate riding coat and held it out to her. "We're probably about the same size," she said.

Cara jumped off Lucas and tried on the coat. It was long in the sleeves for her and a little broad across the back, but apart from that it was fine.

"Thank you," she said with a sigh of relief. "This will do the trick."

"I hope it brings you luck," said Ms. P., smiling. "Now please, get back to warming up that horse."

"I'd love to," Cara answered. Mounting quickly, she rode off to the practice jumps.

There were about thirty finalists, of all different ages, although Cara and Vicki were definitely the youngest. Cara was scheduled to ride toward the end, and Vicki in the middle.

When Vicki's turn came, the nervousness Merlin had shown earlier finally burst out of control. At the water jump he refused three times and was disqualified. Fighting back tears of disappointment, Vicki cantered out of the ring.

"That's a shame," Cara said to Ms. P.

Ms. P. nodded. "We'll talk about it later," she said. "Prepare yourself for your ride."

Taking deep breaths, Cara waited, meticulously going through the course in her mind. She didn't want to see anybody or talk to anybody—she just wanted to be alone with Lucas. Rubbing his neck, she whispered words of encouragement, and finally she was as calm as he was.

When it was her turn, she entered the ring. She was aware of a flutter in the spectators' area but kept her eyes firmly on the jumps. She approached the vertical at a tight angle, giving Lucas his head only as the jump came up to meet them. He cleared it magnificently and cantered eagerly on to the next jump. In a whirl of speed and energy they thundered over the course, soaring over verticals, oxers, and combinations; steadying and pulling back for the combinations—doubles and triples that took her breath away.

Lucas loved it! Ears pricked, tail swishing, eyes

alert, he was perfectly in his element. Cara felt her throat tighten a couple of times: when she really thought they wouldn't make the tight, tight turn into the triple combination or, worse still, when a pole wobbled on the fourth fence. Breathing deep, forcing herself to be calm, she prepared herself for the dreaded wall. Suddenly it loomed. This time she was determined not to lose her nerve.

"Go for it, boy!" she whispered. Lucas kept up his speed, but she had him firmly in check, only letting him go when she felt the lift of his front legs as the jump came up to meet them.

"Clear round for number thirty-three."

"You wonderful, wonderful horse!" cried Cara, rapturously patting Lucas's sweating neck.

As she cantered out, Ms. P. ran toward her.

"You're the sixth to go clear. Well done."

The final entrant went clear too, and then the judge announced the order of the jump-off. Cara was again at the end of the line. The course was quickly rearranged with only seven fences, but they were high, tight, and extremely difficult. Cara gulped nervously. Would they make it through this time?

As she stood outside the ring, tensely watching the other riders race against the clock, Cara noticed that everybody missed on the triple.

"I must get his strides right," she muttered to herself as her name was called.

"Number thirty-three. Cara Zol on Erin's Luck."

Cantering Lucas around, waiting for the bell to sound, Cara was vaguely aware of many smiling, expectant faces turned in their direction, but her attention was focused on the course. When the bell rang, she zoomed Lucas over the vertical, one of the simpler jumps, and then firmly gathered him in for the triple combination. She steadied him for the first fence. They cleared it, but Lucas landed heavily. Keeping his stride and maintaining their rhythm, Cara took him over the second part of the triple, landing a little farther forward than she'd anticipated. Holding her breath, she pulled hard on the reins to position him and then urged him on with her legs almost as the third part of the jump was on top of them. Over he went, with a mighty surge of grace and muscle, clearing the jump spectacularly.

Cara felt like shouting for joy, but there were still more jumps to clear, including the water jump. Feeling Lucas accelerate under her, she checked him for the next combination. Just around the corner was the water jump. When she'd studied it earlier, she'd assumed it was a routine width; coming onto it now, from a left- hand turn, it looked immensely wide. As they took off, Cara wondered if they'd actually make it to the other side.

Lucas clearly had no such forebodings. Opening out like a jackknife, he soared the distance, landing so heavily that Cara shot inches out of the saddle. Laughing with triumph, she cantered around, trying to get both of them back under control.

"Number thirty-three, Erin's Luck. Clear round in fifty-one seconds."

Cara didn't need anyone to tell her who was the

118

winner. Punching the air, she cantered over to a beaming Ms. P.

"You were magnificent!" she shouted. "Stunning! An excellent performance."

Cara kept shaking her head in disbelief. "Thanks," she murmured, tears filling her eyes. "Thank you for everything!"

"My pleasure, I assure you," Ms. P. said proudly. "Shh!" she said, lifting her hand. "They're announcing the results."

Cara held her breath.

"The results of the Culpeper regional finals. In first place . . ." There was a pause that nearly drove Cara crazy. "Number thirty-three, Erin's Luck, ridden by Cara Zol, owned by Mrs. Lucille Deneuve."

"Yay!" Cara screamed, and throwing herself out of the saddle, she hugged both Ms. P. and Lucas simultaneously.

"In second place is . . ." The results continued, giving Cara time to catch her breath before Mrs. Deneuve bore down on her like an overexcited rhinoceros. She praised Lucas to the skies, hardly mentioning Cara, who didn't dare take Lucas away from the admiring throng even though she was a little worried about him getting cold. Fortunately Ms. P. said to Mrs. Deneuve in her best hearty manner, "We'd better get your wonderful animal cooled off before we take him home."

Mrs. Deneuve nodded. Right now *nothing* was good enough for Lucas.

"Certainly! I was just about to suggest that myself," she replied as she fluttered off, leaving Sophie behind.

"I've never seen anything like it!" Sophie gasped, her eyes wide with wonder and pride. "You just sailed through that course. It was the most beautiful thing I've ever seen."

Cara's smiling face froze as Vanessa loomed behind her sister, her face twisted with hate.

"Thanks to you we're stuck in this hole!" she snarled. "As long as you and that rotten horse keep Mom happy, we'll *never* go back to D.C." Her voice dropped to a threatening whisper. "I'm through with your having fun at *our* expense. One way or another, I'm going to put a stop to your free ride—do you understand?"

Cara gulped. Looking at Vanessa's venomous face, her eyes flashing hatred, Cara had no trouble understanding *exactly* what she meant.

12

THE NEXT WEEK, THE THING CARA WANTED MOST IN THE world happened: Vanessa went away. Unfortunately Sophie went too.

"I'll be back after Easter," Sophie said.

"I know," Cara said glumly.

"Think positive. At least you won't have Vanessa breathing down your neck for ten whole days."

"Yeah, but I'll still miss you," Cara said.

"I'll miss you too," Sophie said, smiling shyly. "And Lucas," she added, holding out a hand laden with carrots.

There were, however, big advantages to being left on her own, Cara thought. With their win at the regionals, she and Lucas had qualified for the national show-jumping finals, scheduled for May 8 in Washington. The finals would require a lot of serious thought and training, plus she would have piles of homework and placement tests when school started again. Cara hadn't done any schoolwork during the vacation, so she had even more to catch up with than usual.

She also managed to see something of Tansy over the vacation. Tansy had been out of town almost every weekend with her parents, caring for a sick grandmother. Over soft drinks and cookies at the Millers' house, Tansy listened in amazement as Cara poured out her adventures.

"I can't believe anybody could be *that* mean!" she gasped after Cara had recited the long list of Vanessa's dirty tricks.

"She can," Cara replied grimly. She glanced up to check the time on the kitchen clock. "Sorry, I've got to go," she said, grabbing her knapsack and coat. "I'll miss the bus."

"Oh, Cara! Just as we were having a good talk," Tansy complained. "I hardly ever get to see you these days."

"I know," Cara admitted. "I'm sorry. But we *will* have fun soon."

"How soon?"

"After the finals," Cara promised.

"Right!" Tansy said with a snort.

Training was easier now that spring, warm and green, had come to stay. Lucas spent nights out in the paddock now instead of in his stall unless the weather turned wet and chilly; then Cara always made sure she brought him in before she went home. Much as Lucas loved the new, tender grass, he always looked up expectantly at Cara's step and never failed to amble across the field to meet her.

"Hi, buddy!" she called every day. "Ready for work?"

Their private lessons with Ms. P. were still officially once every two weeks, but now Ms. P. turned up every Sunday afternoon. Cara worried about not paying her for the extra lesson, but her teacher wouldn't hear of it.

"You can pay me back when you're on the international show-jumping circuit," she always teased.

Cara could only smile and thank her, but she vowed to herself that if she ever did get rich, she'd pay Ms. P. back every cent. And Cara knew she didn't just owe her money: Ms. P. gave her time and endless support. She could hardly compare the Ms. P. she knew and loved to the battle-ax she'd been terrified of less than a year ago.

However, although Ms. P. might have softened to Cara as a person, as a rider she was harder on her than ever. The training program she organized for Cara over the Easter vacation was grueling. The jumps moved up and down, changing in height from day to day, and were always varied and challenging.

"Can't have you falling asleep," said Ms. P. "If you always expect a four-foot jump, you'll be careless when you're faced with a three foot nine."

Cara, who had just stupidly knocked down a three foot six, agreed wholeheartedly. "I don't know which I'm most worried about, the three foot six or the four foot six," she said, only half joking.

"See it all as a challenge," Ms. P. instructed. "Lucas certainly does!"

Lucas seemed to love the training. He responded to all of it with enthusiasm and curiosity, flying over every course they set up for him. Even Ms. P. openly admired his talent.

"Pegasus!" she cried after he zipped over a course at light speed. "You were made to fly," she added, stroking his mane and neck.

"I wasn't!" gasped Cara.

"He's a powerful boy when he gets excited," said Ms. P., her eyes sweeping over Cara critically as if she were a gangly filly. "You might look small and delicate, but you're as tough as old boots—you can handle him!"

Cara didn't know whether to take her remark as an insult or a compliment. Ms. P. slapped Lucas's hindquarters and said, "Come along, back to business, both of you."

With aching limbs, Cara continued her training, which that day focused on lengthening and shortening Lucas's stride on approaches to the jumps. As the jumps got bigger Cara realized that she was sticking out her arms and losing the strong line from Lucas's mouth through her hands to her elbows.

"Don't flap!" yelled Ms. P. as Cara went at a jump and her elbows shot up. "He's the one doing the flying—just sit deep!"

Concentrating her thoughts on her elbows, Cara managed to keep them tucked in and push her arms forward in a straight line along his neck, giving him his head.

"Good!" cried Ms. P. "I know it's difficult to remember, but you must keep those elbows in. Otherwise, you'll have the reins all over the place and lose control."

With higher jumps, Cara appreciated the advantage of taking most of her weight off Lucas's back. During flight she needed to push her weight onto her thighs and ankles, lightening his load and letting him soar freely. Unfortunately the impulse when faced with a four-foot-six wall was to sit down deep in the saddle and hold on tight.

"Move *forward*!" Ms. P. shouted at her time and again.

After an hour of being corrected, Cara was pushing forward automatically, even though her thigh muscles screamed in agony. By the third week of training she felt very tired, but her leg muscles were finally in shape.

"Don't overdo it," warned Ms. P. "You're progressing nicely."

As Cara's jumping became more confident, Ms. P. took her through various course formations, theoretically to start with, then practically.

"Take a look at this," she said one day out in the paddock, opening a sketch of a Grand Prix course she'd drawn up. "Last year's final was almost identical to this."

Cara gulped when she saw how complicated the layout of the course was. "It's huge!" she gasped.

"Because it's an outdoor event, the course has a nice open feel," Ms. P. continued calmly. "Almost like a cross-country course. I'm sure you'll enjoy it."

Cara smiled weakly. "I hope so," she said.

"The turns are tight and intricate; they might cause a problem unless you bend and dip very quickly. Lucas is no Arab—he can't double back on himself as fast as one, but he is supple and very clever."

Lucas stuck his head over her shoulder and nudged her.

"Go eat some grass," said Ms. P., patting him affectionately on the neck. "We're talking about serious matters." Lucas blew into her hair and trotted off. "Obviously you'll walk the course and pace it," continued Ms. P. "But I want you to be ready for these turns. I don't want them throwing you into a panic at the last minute."

Ms. P. frequently rearranged the jumps, testing Cara by taking her out of a triple-bar oxer on a sharp right turn and straight into a vertical. Cara had learned months ago to stop Lucas from jumping big over oxers, causing them to land too far on the other side to be in stride for another jump immediately following. If she lost her concentration or forgot to give him room to lighten his forehand, then he inevitably put more weight on his hindquarters to jump the vertical out and the jump couldn't be as high. In the past Cara had occasionally gotten away with mistakes— Lucas was such an excellent jumper, he could finesse most situations—but on a grueling course like the finals any mistake would be fatal.

126

Cara worked on all her shortcomings, and Ms. P. schooled her almost to death. Finally Cara felt she was ready for the Olympics!

"If only the show were tomorrow," she said after she and Lucas had stunningly completed a course in record time.

"Well, it isn't," said Ms. P. "It's three weeks away, and you're going back to school on Tuesday."

Cara groaned. "It's not going back to school that worries me, though," she said.

"Oh?" Ms. P. looked intently at Cara's face. "What is it, then?"

"The Deneuves come home tomorrow."

Ms. P. nodded with a grim look. "You leave the mother to me," she said briskly. "She's quite harmless; just a little dimwitted at times."

"Vanessa's not dimwitted," Cara blurted. "She wants me out of here."

Ms. P.'s face creased with concern.

"It's not me I'm worried about," Cara added hastily. "It's Lucas. I sometimes think there's nothing she wouldn't do to get rid of me. . . ." She looked at Ms. P. anxiously.

"Really, somebody ought to sort that girl out," Ms. P. said thoughtfully. "She needs help."

"Yes, but I don't see what anyone can do," Cara said desperately. "If you're nice to Vanessa, it just makes her furious. Sometimes I wish I were invisible, so she'd never even see me at the stables."

Ms. P. smiled and sighed. "I understand how difficult it is for you," she said. "But somebody really

127

should make an effort to understand Vanessa, too."

Cara stared at her in surprise.

"If she doesn't get help," Ms. P. continued, "she's going to get a *lot* worse. Perhaps I should try talking to her mother."

Cara shook her head. "No. Please, wait until after the finals," she begged.

Ms. P. didn't look convinced. "How will you prevent more incidents?" she asked.

"I've got Sophie," Cara reminded her. "She's a good friend. We look after each other these days." Cara smiled, thinking how strange it was that she and Sophie had become so close and protective of each other. "I'm lucky, really," she added brightly.

"Well, let's hope your luck holds out till May 8," Ms. P. replied.

Sophie came back from Washington happy and bubbling.

"I had the greatest time with my dad," she said when she found Cara in the feed room. "But I did miss Lucas a lot, and you too." Shyly, she handed Cara a present. "It's a little late, but happy Easter."

Cara unwrapped the bright, sparkly paper and stopped, astonished. "Oh, it's beautiful!" she cried. Sophie had framed a picture of Lucas at the Culpeper show. He was soaring over the water jump, perfectly extended, his eyes bright with excitement.

"I took the photograph," said Sophie proudly. "I had it enlarged and bought the frame in D.C."

"It's wonderful!" said Cara, truly touched by her friend's generosity.

"I got one for me too," Sophie admitted.

"Did you hang it over your bed?" Cara teased.

Sophie shook her head. "I don't dare," she said. "Vanessa would stick it in the trash right away."

"That's a shame. I was hoping she might come back in a better mood," said Cara.

"Dream on," said Sophie. "She's worse than ever. She's been giving Mom an awful time."

"I'm going to ask you a really hard question and I want you to answer me honestly," Cara said, staring at Sophie. "Do you think Vanessa would go as far as actually hurting Lucas?"

Sophie thought for a minute. "In the city, with Dad and her boyfriend, she was completely normal. Here"—she shook her head—"she changes into a monster." She looked Cara straight in the eyes. "There's no telling what will happen."

Cara sat on a sack of oats. "I don't know what to do," she murmured, half to herself. "I'll go crazy if she lays a finger on Lucas."

"I'll look after him when you're not around," Sophie promised.

"What would I do without you?" Cara cried, hugging Sophie tight.

"We're friends," said Sophie, her face bright. "We'll look after each other—and Lucas too!"

Fortunately nothing happened to Lucas during the first week back at school. Cara began to feel guilty for badmouthing Vanessa, whom she hadn't seen for over a month, and even hopeful that she might have

129

reformed. But when Vanessa finally turned up in the stable yard, just as Sophie was finishing her riding lesson with Ms. P., Cara realized she had no reason to feel guilty for thinking anything awful about Vanessa.

"Who would have thought a boring, dumpy girl like Sophie would take to the saddle?" she said.

Cara kept quiet. The last thing she wanted was to antagonize Vanessa, who was staring at her with a truly evil expression.

"And how's the little hillbilly enjoying my mother's open checkbook?" she asked.

Cara swallowed to control her anger. "Your mother's very generous with *Lucas*," she said pointedly.

"Too generous with a user like you," Vanessa snapped.

Cara resented Vanessa's accusation, after all she'd done for Mrs. Deneuve with Lucas. "Your mother has a business arrangement with me, that's all," she said coldly.

"Sure!" sneered Vanessa. "She gives and you take. Why don't you get your own horse?"

Cara flinched as the words stung, but turned away. No matter how much Vanessa's tormenting hurt, she had no intention of letting Vanessa see it.

Vanessa poked her hard in the back. "Just in case you think I mellowed out since my vacation in D.C.— I haven't!" Her voice dropped to a threatening whisper and her dark eyes flashed dangerously. "You won't make that final, country girl. Okay?"

Cara shivered involuntarily. "Vanessa," she began

reasonably, "I don't ride Lucas just to annoy *you*. Your mother asked me to event him, and I do my best. He's the talented one, not me."

"Then you better try *less* hard," Vanessa hissed. "Otherwise I'll have to think of something that will really cramp your style." With a snarl Vanessa turned abruptly and stomped back to the house. Cara realized she was shaking all over from fear and anger. Ms. P. found her in the tack room, white and still shaking, at the end of Sophie's lesson.

"Vanessa?" Ms. P. asked.

Cara nodded. This time, she had no intention of playing the solitary hero. Vanessa's threats were too much for her to handle alone.

"She's just said that she'll stop me from taking Lucas to the finals."

Ms. P. looked furious. "Does Mrs. Deneuve have *any* idea what's going on?" she asked.

Cara shook her head. "She just thinks Vanessa doesn't like Virginia."

Ms. P. whacked her whip against the door and muttered something Cara was sure she wasn't supposed to hear. Sophie walked into the tack room with Lucas's saddle.

"Would it help if I talked to your mother?" Ms. P. asked her.

"It might," Sophie said cautiously. "If Mom can keep what you say to herself. If she blabs it to Vanessa, Cara will be in even bigger trouble."

Ms. P. strode off to the farmhouse, leaving the girls with the jitters.

131

"What did you mean about your mom keeping her mouth shut?" Cara asked anxiously.

"When she's mad, Mom says the first thing that comes into her head," Sophie explained.

Cara groaned.

"Maybe just this once she'll be subtle," said Sophie, obviously forcing herself to be optimistic.

Cara shrugged. She wasn't convinced.

Later that afternoon, just as she was leaving the stables, Mrs. Deneuve came out of the house and stopped her on the drive.

"I hear you've been having some problems," she said.

Cara looked around nervously. The last thing she wanted was for Vanessa to see her talking to Mrs. Deneuve.

"You must understand Vanessa's not happy in the country," said Mrs. Deneuve with her sweetest smile. "It might take her some time to settle in."

Cara gulped. Was Mrs. Deneuve that blind? "There's more to it than that," she said boldly. "Vanessa seriously doesn't want me around here."

Mrs. Deneuve smiled brightly. "I know. She's terribly jealous," she answered. "But I've told her somebody has to exercise Lucas, and until either she or Sophie can manage it, you'll *have* to be around." Cara felt like a disposable object.

Mrs. Deneuve steamed on. "She's probably feeling out of it now that Sophie's doing so well with her riding, but I'm sure she'll change her ways—especially after the finals."

She's completely missed the point, Cara thought as she rode home on the bus, her mind boiling with anxiety.

The following school week, all the eighth-graders had placement tests, so Cara was busy all day and every evening studying. Sophie's school hadn't scheduled tests for that week, and so she volunteered to ride Lucas every night after school.

"I won't jump him," she added as a joke, but Cara didn't laugh. Instead she said, "Your riding's coming along really well. You'll be jumping him in three months, believe me."

By Thursday night Cara's nerves were shot. Instinct told her that *something* was wrong. She didn't dare phone Sophie in case Vanessa answered, and it was far too late to catch a bus over there. She tried to study, but every nerve in her body was jangling.

When the phone rang, Cara pounced on it like a cat. It was Sophie, breathless and almost in tears.

"Vanessa came down to Lucas's stall tonight," she whispered. "She started teasing me and messing around . . ." Her voice trailed off.

"Messing with *what*?" Cara asked.

"Not Lucas, I made sure of that," Sophie answered staunchly. "I put him out in the paddock and left him there, too."

Cara let out a long sigh of relief. As long as Lucas was safe nothing else much mattered.

"She started playing around with his saddle," Sophie continued. "Then she grabbed his bridle from me, took some scissors, and cut the reins in half."

Cara was angry but kept her temper. "We'll just have to get them fixed right away," she said practically.

"But there's more!" cried Sophie. Cara had a sick feeling there would be.

"She says if I don't stop hanging out with you, she'll finish our friendship once and for all." The tears Sophie had been trying to suppress suddenly flowed. "She said she'd get Lucas next time!" Sophie sobbed wildly.

"Do you think she'll do it?"

"Yes!" cried Sophie, sounding terrified.

"Then we won't take any chances. We'll watch her every second, day and night," said Cara grimly. "We've got to be ahead of her all the time, predicting her movements for the next eight days."

"Right," Sophie agreed.

Friday dragged on at school, but at least the achievement tests were finally over. That afternoon Cara took the bus to the farmhouse and found Lucas perfectly fine, grazing serenely in the paddock.

"Hi, boy!" she called. "You look like you're having a nice quiet time." Whinnying softly, he trotted up to her and blew in her hair. Cara led him into the stable, crosstied him in the aisle, and quickly groomed him and tacked him up. She felt her troubles roll away as they set off at a brisk trot across the ring to the course Ms. P. had set up the previous weekend.

As Cara approached the course she realized that something was strange about it. The jumps were there—the verticals and oxer spreads—but nearly all the poles and planks were gone. She frantically cantered around the course, checking each jump. At least a dozen were incomplete.

Suddenly she remembered that she had smelled fire since she had arrived at the stables this afternoon. The gardener usually burned the garden refuse near evening. Turning Lucas, she galloped up the drive toward the fire and saw her worst fears confirmed. Crackling away were the last remains of the red-and-white parallel poles, their paint hissing as the flames licked around them.

"Oh, no," Cara groaned, dropping her head into her hands. Reins could probably be fixed; half a show-jumping course was another story altogether. She slowly returned to the stable yard and found Sophie, late in getting back from school. Sophie's smile of greeting vanished when she saw Cara's expression.

"What now?" she gasped.

"Someone burned half the jumps," Cara said, nodding toward the distant fire. "Whoever it was must have been pretty determined to haul them all the way down there."

"What are we going to do?" asked Sophie, clearly shaken.

"I can ride Lucas over at Ms. P.'s stable," said Cara. "She's got—"

"I meant about Vanessa. She's going totally crazy. Cara, she's dangerous," Sophie added in a terrified whisper.

You're not telling me anything new, Cara thought.

Aloud she said, "I'm going to stay with Lucas *all* day and *all* night."

"What about your parents?" Sophie asked. "What will you tell them?"

"I'll tell them the truth—I'm staying with you."

"At the house?" Sophie asked incredulously.

"No, here," Cara said with a grin. "You and I will be sleeping in the tack room—together!"

It was a long, hard weekend for Cara. Each day she walked Lucas over to Ms. P.'s stable, took her lesson and hacked back, then spent the night on hay bales. Sophie stayed with Cara as long as possible each night, then slipped back to the house to avoid arousing suspicion.

The first two nights passed uneventfully. Just when Cara was beginning to think she'd overreacted, she got her next big scare.

She was dozing on the hay bales, hidden in a dark corner of the tack room, when suddenly she heard someone prowling around the stable yard. From the doorway Cara watched Vanessa creep down the aisle and open Lucas's stall door. Lucas gave a surprised snort. Vanessa cautiously approached him and gingerly patted his neck. Lucas stood quietly, even though he had just been jarred from a sound sleep. Vanessa fingered his long mane, then left just as quickly as she'd come.

Sighing with relief, Cara slumped against the wall, her heart pounding. After a moment she got up and walked into Lucas's stall, where she examined him carefully.

"Are you all right, buddy?" she whispered. Lucas stamped his foot and bumped his nose against her chest. "Oh, Lucas!" she cried despairingly. "I wish she'd leave us alone."

Lucas huffed gently into her hair, and Cara felt a little comforted. "Good night, sweetheart," she said, gently removing a wisp of straw from his forelock and kissing his nose. "I'll be right here with you."

Cara crept back to the hay bales, where she settled down, but not to sleep. She tossed and turned for hours, then finally fell into a troubled sleep in which she dreamed Vanessa was running away with Lucas. As Cara gave chase, the paddock changed into a barren moonscape and Lucas disappeared down a swirling black hole. Cara woke up in a sweat. *"Lucas!"* she screamed. Then she realized groggily it had just been a dream. Tired and aching all over, she got up and watched the dawn break over the line of hazy blue hills. The farmhouse lay in a drift of mist, and the birds sang a joyful spring chorus.

"It all looks so peaceful," she said with a sigh. But she knew better than anyone that neither she nor Lucas would have any real peace until next Saturday—when the finals would at last be over.

13

CARA STARTED THE WEEK TIRED AND STRAINED, BUT IT WAS
worth it to protect Lucas. During the week she
couldn't keep watch the entire night, but she stayed
with him until the last bus went at eight thirty, then
Sophie stood guard until about eleven.

All went well until Friday, the day before the finals, when the worst came to pass. Cara went to the
farmhouse after school, but Lucas wasn't out in the
paddock, as he usually was. Her heart in her throat,
she ran to the stable and found Lucas tied up in his
stall. His beautiful mane had been cropped and lay in
a drift of gold around his feet.

"Oh, my God!" she cried. Flinging open his door,
she rushed in and stared wildly around, unable to believe that *anybody*—even Vanessa—could do such a
hideous thing.

Shaking his head in a very puzzled manner, Lucas
nudged her arm.

"It's all right, boy," she said, choking back angry tears.

Not daring to leave him alone for a second, Cara waited an hour for Sophie, who always got back from school much later than she did. In that hour Cara made a momentous decision: she was going to put an end to this cruelty, once and for all.

"What *happened*?" Sophie shrieked when she saw Lucas, her eyes wide with horror.

"Later," Cara said. "Would you watch him? I have to go home."

When she walked into the kitchen, she found her parents and brother finishing supper.

"Mom, Dad." Cara swallowed hard as tears threatened. "I need your help."

She sat between her parents, and the whole ghastly story came pouring out. Her parents listened tight-lipped, clearly shocked by the sequence of disasters she'd endured.

"Why on earth didn't you tell us earlier?" asked her mother, her face pale.

"If I'd told you, would you have let me keep going over there?" Cara asked.

"No," her father said truthfully.

"There's only one more day till the finals, then it's all over—"

"Until the next time," Mrs. Zol added.

"No, Mom. There *can't* be a next time; this has to be the *last* time." Cara couldn't hold back her tears as she talked. "I've made up my mind—this has got to stop. It's too dangerous for Lucas."

"And you too, honey," Mr. Zol said, stroking her dark hair.

"I don't care about *me*!" she cried. "It's Lucas I'm worried about."

"You worry about Lucas and leave us to worry about you," her father said gently.

"Will you help me?" she asked, squeezing their hands tight. "This last time?"

"You know we will," Mr. Zol answered.

"What do you want us to do?" asked her mother.

"The more people I have guarding Lucas, day and night, the less chance Vanessa has of getting near him."

Her parents nodded in agreement.

"Dad, will you guard him tonight? Then I can get some sleep before the finals."

"I'd be glad to, sweetie."

"Mom can drive me over to the stables at dawn, and maybe I can leave for Washington before anybody in the house knows I'm even there. Is that okay, Mom?"

"Sounds like a good plan," said Mrs. Zol.

"All right," said Mr. Zol, quickly finishing his coffee. "What do I need for a night out with Lucas?"

"Earmuffs!" Cara teased. "He snores."

Cara felt much better after her dad had left. She made a list of things left to do and systematically went through it. She laid out her riding outfit, polished her boots, and pressed the show-jumping coat Vicki Wolfe had lent her.

"I won't be needing it," she had said sadly. "But I

hope it brings you luck in the finals."

Before she went to bed, Cara telephoned the driver of the horse van—just to make sure no one had canceled it. She also asked him to pick her up at eight instead of nine. The sooner she got out of Vanessa's way, the better.

Around eleven the phone rang. It was Sophie.

"I can't talk for long," she whispered nervously. "Mom's in a towering rage. She and Van have been arguing all night."

"How's Lucas?" Cara asked anxiously.

"He's fine, just fine," Sophie assured her. "Your dad's down there prowling around. He'll frighten anybody away."

Cara smiled to herself at the thought of her dad creeping around the stable with Lucas watching him.

"What about the tack?" she asked. "Have you locked it up?"

"Yes, in my blanket chest along with the leg wraps, and I've got the key under my mattress," Sophie answered with a giggle.

"Brilliant! You've thought of everything," said Cara.

"So, you can relax. Get some sleep, and I'll see you tomorrow," Sophie whispered. The receiver clicked.

Suddenly exhaustion caught up with Cara. The tension of the last week hit her hard, and she felt staggeringly tired. Forcing herself to keep her eyes open for another ten minutes, she flicked through her horse manual until she came to the section on plaiting manes. She carefully studied the different techniques she could use on Lucas's shorn mane. Vanessa might think she'd ruined Lucas's good looks, but Cara intended to make sure that the next day Lucas looked just as beautiful as ever!

Cara's alarm went off at five. After a quick breakfast Mrs. Zol drove her over to the stable, where they found Mr. Zol fast asleep in Lucas's stall.

"I got nervous about leaving him," he explained. "So I settled down in here with him. He didn't seem to mind a bit."

"Thanks, Dad," Cara said, hugging him close. "Now go home and get some real sleep."

"I will," said Mr. Zol, with a huge yawn. "You never told me how itchy straw is!" he added, pulling out wisps from under his shirt collar.

"See you at the show, honey," said Mrs. Zol, kissing Cara's forehead. "Stay calm."

"I will now that I have my bodyguards," Cara said gratefully.

As soon as they'd gone she turned her attention to Lucas. "Let's see what I can do with that mane of yours!"

Lucas stood patiently while she groomed him and then set to work on his mane. It had been hacked haphazardly, so the first thing she did was trim it all to the same length. Then she plaited it into tiny gold strips, finishing each with a tight twist of a red rubber band. Her heart ached for the silky luxuriance of his former mane, but when she stood back to check him over, she was pleasantly surprised by how good he looked.

"Stylish," she said admiringly. Lucas shook his head as if he were trying out the new mane for style too.

Sophie dropped by the stable about seven thirty and was very impressed by the new look. "Nobody would ever know he just had eight inches chopped off his mane," she said.

Sophie had brought the tack and leg wraps that she had locked overnight in her blanket chest. "All in good shape," she said, and began to help Cara wrap Lucas's legs.

"I asked the driver to come at eight," said Cara, dropping her voice to a whisper. "I thought the sooner we were away from here, the better."

Sophie nodded. "Good thinking, Batman!" she said with a giggle.

When Lucas was ready, they walked him into the stable yard. There, in the quiet of the May morning, Cara told Sophie of her decision. "This is going to be the last time I'll ever ride Lucas for your mother," she said.

Sophie stared at her in astonishment.

"It's too dangerous for Lucas," Cara continued. "That's pretty obvious, isn't it?"

Sophie seemed about to say something; then she sighed and nodded. "Yes. I don't want Lucas to get hurt any more than you do." Then she burst out, "Oh, Cara! I'll miss you."

Fortunately the van rolled into view at that moment, leaving no time for tears. Sophie helped Cara load Lucas, then hugged her tight. "Good luck," she said. "You deserve success!"

The highways weren't crowded, but it was still a long drive to Washington. Just outside the city, road repairs were causing chaos on most of the major routes.

"Good thing we left early," said the driver as they joined a long traffic jam.

Cara was anxious to get to the showgrounds and walk the course before Mrs. Deneuve and Vanessa arrived. She'd been hoping that chopping off Lucas's mane would have satisfied Vanessa and she wouldn't show up for the finals, but no such luck. Sophie told her that Mrs. Deneuve was forcing Vanessa to go, threatening to ground her if she didn't.

We just don't seem to get any lucky breaks, Cara thought gloomily. *I wish for a change something would happen to help us.* The final was scheduled for two that afternoon. They arrived just after twelve, but the showgrounds were already teeming with people. Cara had read on her entry form that there were thirty-three competitors.

What are all these people doing here? she wondered. Suddenly it hit her—they were spectators! There to watch and have a good day out. Feeling her stomach churn as if she were on a Ferris wheel, Cara asked the driver if he would stay with Lucas while she checked in. She stopped by the show office and was given her number: eight.

Eight on May 8, she thought. *Maybe that's a lucky sign—or am I being silly?*

Cara walked toward the course. It was just as Ms.

P. had described it. The combinations were daunting, and she hadn't exaggerated at all about the deadly turns. Pacing them out, Cara realized there wasn't room for *any* mistakes. Each turn had to be perfectly accurate or Lucas would lose his stride and she would certainly lose her rhythm. Some of the four-foot-six combinations looked massive, as did the oxer, which she calculated they could take more quickly after a left turn. If she wanted to pick up speed points, that was the most direct way to go.

Ms. P. had been right about the layout—it did have a lovely open-air feel to it, like a cross-country course. The jumps were bright against the emerald grass and clean blue sky. A rain shower the night before had made the ground soft but not soggy, and there was a light breeze blowing—it was a perfect day for show jumping!

Cara walked back to the van, feeling much calmer, and found that Ms. P. had replaced the driver.

"I suggested he might like a sandwich," she said. "Anyway, I wanted to see how Lucas was." She looked pointedly at Cara. "Your mother phoned me early this morning and told me about his mane," she said briskly. "It's best not to get too emotional about it at the moment—he looks splendid anyway. You've done an excellent restoration job."

Cara glowed with pride. If Ms. P. thought Lucas looked good, then he really must!

"Let's get him unloaded," said Ms. P.

Lucas was in his usual preshow mood: excited and immensely pleased with himself. Unfortunately he couldn't toss his silky mane anymore, but nothing could stop him from whinnying shrilly to announce his arrival.

"You don't need a fanfare," said Ms. P. with an amused smile.

Cara walked him around on a lead rope, letting him take in the atmosphere and settle down. Just after one o'clock she tacked him up and went into her own preshow mood: quiet, thoughtful, and slightly withdrawn.

"I'll keep an eye on the van while you put him through his paces," said Ms. P., and added jokingly, "I'll make sure no one puts frogs in his water bucket!"

Cara thanked her and set off at a brisk trot, suddenly incredibly happy. The past few weeks had been a nightmare, and the future held no promises, but *this* moment with Lucas was perfect. She was as ready for the finals as she could possibly be: she had worked to the point where she was practically training in her sleep. If she could keep her nerve, and if fate kept Vanessa out of her way, she stood an excellent chance of doing well. Feeling her cares fly free, she trotted Lucas out of the showgrounds, away from the noise and the clamor, toward the open fields beyond.

As Lucas broke into a canter she realized he was more wound up than normal. Maybe he knew how important a day it was—what was at stake. Lucas opened up into a fast, rollicking canter, then checked himself after about a quarter of a mile, exactly when

146

Cara would have asked him to stop. They walked quietly back to the showgrounds, but Cara almost lost her composure when she saw Mrs. Deneuve waiting by the van with her daughters. Cara almost laughed when she noticed how Ms. P. never took her eyes off Vanessa. She was watching her like a rattlesnake.

"Goodness!" shrieked Mrs. Deneuve, so loudly that Lucas shied. "What have you done to his mane?"

Cara hadn't thought of a convincing excuse for Lucas's new cropped look. "Well," she started.

"We didn't want him to get sweated up," interrupted Ms. P.

Technically this made no sense, although it sounded fairly convincing. Mrs. Deneuve nodded, but Cara saw her eyes flick, just for a second, toward her older daughter.

"I see," she said, too quickly. For the first time Cara had a feeling that Mrs. Deneuve wasn't as stupid as she seemed, and that she knew more about what had been happening with Lucas than she let on.

"Good luck, Lucas!" she said brightly. "We'll be watching for you." Off she glided, with her arm tucked firmly in Vanessa's. Sophie stayed behind, staring anxiously at Lucas.

"Is there anything I can do?" she asked.

"Yes—stay with Lucas while I check to see if my parents are here," Cara said gratefully.

She dashed off, comforted by the wall of supportive friends around her. Vanessa would have to be invisible to get near Lucas this afternoon!

She found her parents with a picnic basket big

enough for ten. Although Mrs. Zol and Mike had been to shows before, the whole family had never been to one together before this.

"This weekend is special," her dad had told her. "I've turned down overtime work. All of us want to be there."

Sophie and Ms. P. joined them for lunch, sitting on the grass beside the van. Cara was too nervous to eat. She nibbled a cracker and half an apple, but food was the last thing on her mind. Her brother's appetite made up for hers. In between mouthfuls he asked nonstop questions about the show.

"Honey, hush," said Mrs. Zol gently. "Cara needs some quiet right now."

"That's okay, Mom," Cara said. "I think it's time to take Lucas over a few practice jumps."

She put him over half a dozen jumps and practiced a few sharp turns. Then she heard the judge announce the start of the show. Joining Ms. P. near the ring, she saw the first competitor canter in.

"At least you won't have a long wait," said Ms. P., noting her entry number.

Cara stayed around to watch the rider tackle the course. He brought down several poles along the way. She glad she didn't have to go first, but she wished it were all over. The knots in her stomach were getting worse by the minute.

"Don't rush it," advised Ms. P. "Don't look at the clock—don't even think about it. Just concentrate on a clear round."

"Okay," said Cara, and trotted off to do a few more

practice jumps as number three was called in. By the time her turn came, there hadn't been one clear round.

"Number eight, Erin's Luck, ridden by Cara Zol, owned by Mrs. Lucille Deneuve," the announcer's voice crackled. Cara cantered in and waited for the starting bell, mentally going through the first few jumps: the vertical poles, clean and welcoming, on to a plank combination, and then to the crossed poles.

Suddenly the bell sounded. As Lucas's ears pricked, adrenaline flooded Cara's body. Leaning forward, she urged Lucas on, cautious in her approach as she neared the inviting first fence. He was over in a shot and heading on a curve for the plank combination. Cara shortened his stride just before takeoff, getting him exactly in the right place for good clearance. Next came the crossed poles, which he flew over.

Then she checked him hard for the turn into the first gate, counting his strides like they were her own heartbeats. When the gate was coming up to meet them, she gave him his head and threw her weight forward. She felt herself lift into the air as he soared and dropped down lightly.

The triple combination was straight ahead. As he cleared the first part she checked his stride, *knowing* he'd make the second and third parts. His timing was magic! The oxer spread loomed next, massive and on the tricky turn that she hadn't liked when pacing out the course. Pulling Lucas back, she shortened his stride for the turn and sat as deep and upright as she could.

149

The crowd grew quiet. Then, as she flew over the spread, she heard a collective sigh of relief. Another plank combination led to a white gate, followed by a forty-five-degree turn for the wall. Excitement was getting the better of Lucas. Cara could feel him accelerating under her and pulling the reins through her hands, trying to get his head.

"Not now," she muttered, hauling back on the reins. She held him tight until he found his stride, and then she let him go for the wall. He was magnificent! But there was no time for jubilating—the triple-bar oxer was coming up. She took the corner just before it with a sharp thrust, giving Lucas the momentum he needed to get his canter in stride. He floated over it!

Cara could feel the crowd behind her and sense their anticipation. It heightened her determination to win. The double combination coming up needed the tightest of strides in between. Shortening Lucas's stride just before takeoff helped her control him on landing between the bars. He gave the stride she needed and they were clear over the second part of the jump.

Next vertical poles led to the water jump. *Only two to go,* thought Cara. *But they're two of the hardest jumps on the course.*

She let Lucas have his head for the vertical and then gathered him in tight on landing. Suddenly, out of the corner of her eye, she saw something wobble. *No!* she thought. But she had to keep her eyes firmly on the water jump, stretching like a river before her.

Although the wobbling jump had broken her concentration, Lucas found his stride without direction and soared over the final jump! The audience applauded wildly.

"Clear round for number eight," a voice said over the loudspeaker.

Feeling giddy with happiness, Cara cantered out of the ring—they were the first with a clean round! Ms. P. was there, punching the air joyfully, and in minutes a crowd had gathered around her and Lucas. Cara pushed through them, away from the ring, so as not to get in the way of the other competitors. As she walked Lucas across the grounds, Mrs. Deneuve found them.

Cara was relieved to see that Vanessa was not in tow this time. Introducing Vanessa to her parents would have been very tricky. Mrs. Deneuve nodded politely at the Zols, but she was too wrapped up in showing Lucas off to her friends to pay them any further attention.

"My wonderful horse," she kept saying. "My wonderful, wonderful horse!"

"Wonderful or not, this horse needs calming down before the jump-off," Ms. P. interrupted. "Another horse just went clean, and probably more will."

Cara quickly turned Lucas, intending to walk him back to the peace and quiet of the van area.

"Don't forget, you're not through," Ms. P. warned as she left. "This may be a big jump-off."

"I know," Cara said.

Back at the van, she tied Lucas and covered him

with a light blanket. Then, when everything had been done to see to his comfort, she threw her arms around his neck and hugged him.

"Oh, Lucas, you were *brilliant!*" she said, tears stinging her eyes. He'd been so willing and generous about everything she'd asked him to do. "You've got the spirit of Pegasus!" she whispered, kissing his velvety nose. "And I'm so proud of you."

Feeling weak at the knees from all the excitement, Cara flopped on the grass and gazed at the feathery white clouds drifting overhead. She gave a long sigh. After all the work and troubles, she and Lucas were *almost* there.

When Sophie joined her, both girls exchanged triumphant looks.

"You made it!" Sophie cried.

"Not quite," Cara reminded her with a smile.

After nearly an hour Cara walked Lucas back to the ring, where competitor number twenty-nine was completing the course. *Four more to go; then they'll set up the jump-off,* she thought. Tingling with excitement, she went in search of Ms. P., who told her that eleven riders had clear rounds so far. Soon the loudspeaker crackled with information on the jump-off.

"The order for the jump-off is number eight, number thirteen, number nineteen . . ." There were seven in all.

"I'm first!" gasped Cara. She'd much preferred being last at the Culpeper show.

"That can be good," Ms. P. reasoned. "At least you don't have to watch everybody else go and worry about how your time will compare with theirs."

Cara smiled at her, reassured. Ms. P. smiled back, then cracked her whip hard against her riding boot. "Come along. Let's walk the course."

There were six jumps this time, all four foot six: a gate, a plank vertical, a triple combination, a triple oxer, a double combination, and the water jump.

"Lovely course," said Ms. P. enthusiastically.

"Lovely but very high!" Cara added.

She had no time to walk Lucas. In just ten minutes her name would be called, and she had to take him over the practice jumps first. Lucas took them effortlessly, but Cara wasn't comforted. Desperately wishing somebody else was going before her, Cara cantered into the ring. This time she *knew* Lucas could make the jumps; what she needed now was speed! Giving Lucas his head, then pulling him in and shortening his stride, she went with him on every jump. The air rushed past them as Lucas seemed to take flight, dipping and soaring. The water jump flashed ahead of them. Lucas cruised over it, knees neatly tucked, clearing it by inches. In an unbelievably short time their round was over.

"Clear round, fifty-one seconds."

Cara pulled Lucas to a dead halt and punched the air. Fifty-one seconds was phenomenal!

"That was fast!" said Ms. P., coming to her side with a proud smile.

"That was *wonderful!*" Cara sighed blissfully.

The mounting tension in the warm-up ring was just too much for her and Lucas. Cara took him for a

153

quiet walk on the grounds, listening anxiously to the results of each ride announced over the loudspeaker. In a funny way, she was in no hurry to learn the outcome of the jump-off. Whatever the results, she was finished. Seven months of work had brought her this far with Lucas—but they wouldn't be going further, not while Vanessa Deneuve was around. Loving Lucas meant not exposing him to terrible danger. Suddenly she saw Sophie running toward her.

"Come on!" Sophie yelled. "The last one's going in."

Cara watched, her heart thumping, as the rider did a brilliant clear round but lost critical seconds on the final turn at the water jump. She held her breath and crossed her fingers as the judge's voice boomed over the loudspeaker system.

"The results of the jump-off are, in first place . . ." There was a pause and the sound of shuffling paper over the mike.

Come on, come on! thought Cara, starting to shake.

"Number eight in fifty-one seconds. In second place, number nineteen in fifty-five seconds . . ." The judge continued to read the results, but Cara didn't hear a word. Her face was buried in Lucas's sweating neck, and tears streamed down her cheeks.

"We won, boy!" she kept saying. "*We won!*"

Ms. P. put an arm around her trembling shoulders and whispered, "You made it happen, Cara. *Your* skill and determination, against heavy odds. Don't forget that."

Cara rode Lucas around the ring, proudly leading

154

the lap of honor. A long blue ribbon fluttered on Lucas's bridle, and she held aloft a huge silver trophy. Lucas loved the applause. He tossed his shorn mane and trotted around the ring as if to say, I *knew* we'd win! Mrs. Deneuve turned up for the photographs afterward pink with excitement. Cara maneuvered Lucas next to her and posed. Suddenly Vanessa pushed through the crowd and grabbed Lucas's bridle.

"This is *my* horse!" she cried, yanking hard on his bit. The crowd gasped as she started dragging Lucas forward.

"Leave him alone!" Cara cried.

"Stop that *immediately*!" yelled Ms. P.

"No! He's mine!" Vanessa screamed wildly. Snatching the reins right out of Cara's hands, she twisted hard on the bit. Lucas had more than enough of her rough handling. Whinnying, he reared up, so high he almost fell over backward. Cara was thrown out of the saddle and cracked her head on a nearby post. She slumped to the ground, almost unconscious with pain. She was vaguely aware that people were pushing around her as cameras flashed.

Ms. P. called, "Stand back! Give her air!" But by this time, the crowd was so packed, no one could move.

Mr. Zol elbowed his way through the onlookers and bent over Cara. She lay prone on her back, her face white.

"Call an ambulance!" he yelled.

Sensing the mood of mounting hysteria, Lucas

155

panicked and reared up again, eyes rolling, hooves flashing. He was so frightened, he struck himself with his hind legs.

"Stand back!" commanded Ms. P. This time she didn't wait for people to do as they were told but shoved aside anyone in her way. She caught Lucas's reins.

"It's okay, boy," she soothed. "Shush, you'll be okay. Come on," she whispered as she gently led him away from the chaos.

Mrs. Deneuve held a weeping Vanessa by the neck and was angrily shoving her through the crowd. Vanessa might have achieved what she had set out to, but it seemed to be giving her little pleasure.

Within minutes the ambulance pulled up, and Cara was taken away on a stretcher. She had one last vision of Sophie staring after her, tears streaming down her face and sobbing, "Oh, Van, why did you do it?"

Then Cara blacked out.

14

WHEN CARA CAME TO AGAIN SHE WAS IN A HOSPITAL BED, her head bandaged and her body aching from head to foot.

"Lucas?" she asked weakly.

"He's fine," answered Mrs. Zol, gently stroking Cara's forehead. "You just rest now."

Sleep engulfed Cara once more. It wasn't until the following morning that she actually realized what had happened to her.

"Lucas reared up," her mother explained.

"Yes, I remember that part," Cara said with a grim smile.

"You crashed into a post. The doctor thought you might have fractured your skull, but fortunately you've only got a bad concussion."

"Only," said Cara, tenderly feeling her throbbing head. "What about Lucas?"

"Ms. P.'s going to see him this morning," said Mrs.

Zol. "She promised she'd stop by with the news. But no running around for you, young lady. The doctor said you've got to take it easy for a few weeks."

Later that morning Ms. P. visited. Cara was relieved to see her looking so cheerful.

"Lucas has a swollen tendon," she said. "He'll have to be kept in his stall for a week, maybe more, and completely rest that leg."

Cara sighed. The news could have been much worse.

"By the way," Ms. P. continued. "I saw Mrs. Deneuve this morning, and she asked me to tell you not to visit Lucas anymore. It's too dangerous for all concerned," she finished bluntly.

Cara nodded. "I know," she answered weakly.

When she was alone, she stared up at the blank white ceiling and wept. Of course she couldn't see Lucas at the stables again. She'd made that decision herself, the day before the show when she'd found Lucas in his stall with his mane chopped off. But the finality of it still hurt. What would she do without him? How would she live?

Cara went home the next day. She lay in bed, weak, listless, and depressed, for a whole week. She didn't want to eat, or read, or see anybody, or do anything. Mrs. Zol was worried sick.

"You must try and eat, honey," she said, clearing away another tray of untouched food.

"I can't, Mom. It just sticks in my throat," Cara said, pushing her face into the pillow.

Sophie came to see her. She seemed bright and

cheerful, and she had brought flowers and photographs of the finals. But for all her lively chatter,
Cara knew something was wrong. Sophie had big
dark rings under her eyes, as if she had either been
sleeping badly or crying a lot.

After about half an hour Cara said, "Okay, Sophie.
What's wrong?"

"Nothing," Sophie replied, glancing down and
nervously fiddling with the photographs on her lap.
"Lucas is fine. He'll be back out in the paddock soon,
just like old times."

But Cara knew it *wasn't* like old times—something
was wrong. After Sophie had gone, she fretted herself
into a fever worrying about Lucas.

"Mom, I've got to see him!" she cried.

"You're not strong enough," said Mrs. Zol. "Anyway, you're not allowed to go to the Deneuves'."

"But I'll get worse if I don't see him," Cara begged.
She knew her mother couldn't argue with that. The
more Cara worried about Lucas, the weaker she got.

"Please, Mom?" she coaxed. "If we drove in through
the back gate and parked behind the stable, nobody
would see us. We'd be in and out in ten minutes."

"I'll think about it," Mrs. Zol said with a sigh.

A few days later she reluctantly drove Cara over to
the farmhouse.

"Ten minutes," she said, stopping the car behind
the stables. "I'll stay here and keep a lookout."

Cara shot out of the car and let herself into
Lucas's stall. The minute she saw him, all her fears
slipped away.

"Oh, Lucas," she murmured. "I've missed you!"

He stared at her as if she were a dream, then with a loud whinny hobbled toward her, his front leg still bandaged after his accident.

"How are you?" she whispered, running her hands along his neck and shorn mane. Lucas nuzzled her, his dark, soft eyes puzzled and questioning.

"Did you wonder where I'd disappeared to?" she asked, laying her head against his sweet-smelling neck and patting his muscular shoulders.

"It's all over, buddy," she said. "I can't see you anymore." Lucas snuffled her hair as she wept against him. "Sophie will look after you now," she promised.

She was crying too much to hear the sound of footsteps crossing the yard. Too late, she saw Vanessa's head framed in the stall doorway.

"Aha!" she crowed. "I thought we had a *trespasser*." She said the word with relish. "Your services aren't required anymore, stable girl. Now, will you leave my horse alone, or do I have to call the police and have you thrown off my property?"

Vanessa smiled, obviously enjoying her power. Cara began to tremble with fear and emotional exhaustion. Holding on to Lucas, who had shied at the sight of Vanessa, she tried to speak.

"I just came to—"

Vanessa interrupted her. Snatching up a riding whip, she cracked it against the stall door, startling both Cara and Lucas.

"Get out!" she yelled.

Suddenly Mrs. Zol appeared beside her.

"I'll take that," she said, quickly removing the whip from Vanessa's hands. "Your temper has an unpleasant way of running away with you, and we don't want any more unfortunate accidents, do we?"

Vanessa glared at her, furious. "You're trespassing," she snapped.

"No, we're not," answered Mrs. Zol calmly. "We've just come to pick up Cara's belongings." She held up Cara's tack box. "I'm sure your mother wouldn't mind, would she?" she added pointedly.

Vanessa scowled and flung open the stall door. Lucas nervously backed up. Cara patted him gently and whispered, "Good-bye, buddy. . . ."

Mrs. Zol firmly led Cara out of the stable to the car. Cara crawled into the passenger seat. She could hardly manage to stay upright, much less stop crying, but she was determined that Vanessa would not see her torn apart. Pressing herself into the back of the seat, she kept her head up and her eyes staring straight ahead. The minute they were out of the drive, she burst into tears and sobbed as if her heart would break into a thousand pieces.

The doctor was furious when he saw Cara the next day.

"She's utterly exhausted," he said. "You must keep her in a stress-free environment, Mrs. Zol; otherwise, it will take her months to recover."

This time her mother was a very strict nurse. No more worrying conversations, no visitors, and certainly no secret visits to Lucas. When Cara fretted about him, her mother briskly reminded her that

161

he wasn't her concern anymore.

"Mom! How can you say that?" Cara cried.

"Because I am sick and tired of seeing the Deneuve family abuse you!" Mrs. Zol snapped.

Shaking with anger, she left the room, leaving Cara staring sadly out the open window. It was a perfect summer day in early June. But what good was that without Lucas? For a whole year her life had revolved around him. He'd been her first thought the minute she opened her eyes every morning and her last thought as she closed them at night. The energy and excitement they'd shared in that year had changed her life completely. How could she go back to being what she had been? She didn't even feel like that girl anymore. Her body burned to ride, her fingers itched to feel the reins, and the muscles she'd built up during her months of jumping practice now ached from lack of use. She felt dull, bored, and listless. Even Ms. P. couldn't shake her out of her misery.

"Come ride Fancy," she suggested.

Cara shook her head. "Thank you," she replied. "But not now."

"Why don't you help me at my stable?" Ms. P. tried again. "I need someone with your expertise."

Cara tried to smile, but tears filled her eyes and slipped unchecked down her pale cheeks. "I just can't." She sighed. "Not yet."

It was Lucas she wanted. Only him. When the pain inside her stopped hurting, maybe then she'd be able to ride again. While it was still there, she couldn't go near another horse.

162

Another week went by before she was strong enough to get up, although not to go out. Mrs. Zol said Cara's friends could visit, on condition that they didn't worry her to death by talking about Lucas. Tansy showed up with a bag of grapes, which she ate herself as she went through all the school gossip. Sophie came with a pile of books and more wonderful photographs of Lucas completing the jump-off in the finals. Cara studied them in every detail, hungry for the sight of him.

"I can't believe it's only six weeks since I rode him." Cara frowned. "It feels like a lifetime."

"Now, don't upset yourself," said Mrs. Zol, who was listening in on their conversation from the kitchen.

"How is he?" Cara whispered.

"Fine, just fine!" answered Sophie. "Out in the paddock, enjoying the sunshine."

Cara smiled politely, but she wasn't convinced.

After missing almost a month, Cara went back for the last few days of school before the summer vacation. She was still pale and thin, but glad to be with her friends again.

"Are you coming to the school dance on Friday night?" Tansy asked.

Cara was in no mood for dances, but she didn't want to keep letting Tansy down, and so they went. Cara tried hard to be sociable, but she just couldn't get into it.

"I'm thinking about something else," she apologized to Tansy.

"Honestly, sometimes I think you'd be better off seeing Lucas than moping around the way you do," said Tansy irritably.

"Sure!" Cara said mockingly. "And how do I arrange that—I've been banished from the premises, remember?"

"You can always sneak in," Tansy answered.

"I tried it and got caught and screamed at by Vanessa."

"Then try again and get a life!" Tansy snapped.

Strangely, instead of making Cara angry back, Tansy's words woke a rebellious spirit in her. She'd felt weak and exhausted for weeks, unable to think straight or do anything. Now that she was strong enough to go back to school, see her friends, and even argue with Tansy, she suddenly realized how mopey she'd become.

I'm sick of feeling half alive, she thought as she jounced home on the bus that afternoon. *Why shouldn't I go see Lucas again? Tansy's right. Anything is better than feeling like this for the rest of my life!*

That night in bed she worked out a plan. She'd take the bus from school, get off at the stop after the Deneuves' house, and sneak back through the woods into the paddock. Vanessa and Sophie always got home from their school much later than she did. The only person who might be around was Mrs. Deneuve, and Cara knew better than anybody that she wasn't in the habit of wandering down to the paddock in the afternoon.

Cara vowed to tell no one—it would be her secret,

and hers alone. Thrilled by the thought of seeing Lucas again, she slept soundly and ate an enormous breakfast.

"It's good to see you eating again," Mrs. Zol commented.

Cara blushed. She hated to deceive her mother, who had been so worried about her and nice to her the past month. But seeing Lucas should make her recover even faster.

That day, right after school, she carried out her plan. She got off the bus at the stop after the Deneuves' place and headed into the woods, her heart thumping. A sudden thought that Vanessa might not be at school, that she might even be walking in the woods close by, made Cara shake with nerves. She dropped down and hid under the shelter of the leafy trees until her breathing slowed to normal and her heart stopped beating loud enough to burst. Glancing anxiously around, she scuttled through the bushes like a nervous rabbit, catching her hair and scratching her face on thorns in the underbrush.

At last she reached the paddock. This time her pulse started to hammer for another reason.

"Lucas . . ." she murmured. Sure she could feel his presence, she hurried closer, her eyes eagerly searching the field for him. Suddenly he was there! But the cry that burst from her lips wasn't one of joy but of shock and dismay. Lucas was skin and bones, and his coat was dull. He looked terrible!

"Buddy!" she called softly. His head was up in a flash, his eyes searching the field for her.

165

"Lucas," she called again, anxious to stay under the trees. "Over here!"

Spotting her, he threw back his head and whinnied loudly, then trotted straight toward her. Blissfully they greeted each other. Lucas nuzzled and bumped her, blowing into her hair and nudging her pockets for carrots. Cara patted and stroked him, kissed his nose, and told him all the things that had happened.

"Oh, I've missed you," she murmured, leaning against his warm, strong neck.

She didn't dare stay long, no more than half an hour. Then she dragged herself away.

"I'll come back soon," she whispered into his mane. He nibbled her hand when she patted his nose. "Promise!"

Lucas watched, seeming puzzled, as she slipped under the fence and ran through the woods. She heard him whinny as she disappeared under the trees, as if to say, Come back! Come back!

Leaving him again was like tearing off her own skin, but one thing was clear in her mind—she'd be back to see him again. Nothing would stop her!

All the way home on the bus Cara wondered why no one had told her the truth about Lucas. *Everyone* had said he was fine, making a good recovery, getting back to normal, when in fact he was none of those things. Maybe they'd been trying to protect her, she reasoned, but she was better now. She could cope—it was Lucas who needed care.

She went to see him several times that week and the next, getting more and more worried about his poor condition. He cheered up when he saw her: his eyes were bright and happy, and he loved all the treats she brought. But he didn't have his old sparkle, he was dramatically underweight, and he certainly hadn't recovered from his injury as quickly as he should have.

"It's strange, boy," she said. "We're both weak and depressed." She gently tugged his ears. "But I think you're a lot worse than me."

She had to get good advice from somebody. There was only one person in the world whose judgment she could completely trust when it came to Lucas— Ms. P. On Sunday afternoon she visited Hunters' Riding School and found Ms. P. in the tack room, polishing bits and bridles.

"I've been going to see Lucas," Cara blurted.

Ms. P. didn't bat an eyelid. She hardly looked up. "I thought you might," she answered coolly.

"He looks terrible!" Cara cried. "He's lost an enormous amount of weight, and he's badly out of condition."

"He's been injured, and no one has ridden him for over a month now. What did you expect to find?" asked Ms. P. realistically.

"I want to help him," Cara answered.

"He's not *your* horse to help," Ms. P. pointed out coldly. Cara flinched. "Harsh words, I know, but the truth," Ms. P. said more gently.

Cara's head drooped. "I just love him," she said, and began to cry.

Ms. P. put aside the tack she was cleaning. "We *all*

love Lucas," she said. "He's a very special animal. But while he belongs to Mrs. Deneuve, there's nothing we can do."

"Sometimes I dream of stealing him away," Cara muttered angrily.

"That would be a very foolish thing to do, believe me," said Ms. P. briskly. "As soon as his leg is completely healed Sophie will be able to ride again. That might cheer him up."

Cara didn't look convinced.

"And I'll be able to see him regularly and keep an eye on him," added Ms. P.

"Promise you'll let me know how he's doing?" Cara begged.

"I promise," Ms. P said.

A week later Ms. P. gave Sophie a riding lesson on Lucas. Sophie stopped by Cara's house afterward to report.

"It was good," she said enthusiastically. "Even though I was really nervous to start with. He went well," she added, seeing Cara's anxious expression. "Ms. P. made sure he didn't overwork his leg. We just walked and trotted, nothing else."

"How does he look?" Cara asked.

"Fine," Sophie answered. "Just a little thin."

A little thin, thought Cara. *Oh, right!* Unable to keep her secret to herself a minute longer, she said, "I've seen him, Sophie, and he's not at all fine."

Sophie gulped and stared at Cara. "When?"

"Last week, and the week before *and* the week before," Cara answered. "I sneak in, before you and Vanessa get home from school. I don't know why you never told me the truth," she added irritably.

"Because I knew it would worry you!" Sophie cried. "Isn't that obvious?"

Cara hesitated, then nodded. "Okay, so now we have no secrets from each other. That's something."

Sophie shook her head and blushed bright pink.

"I have a secret," she murmured.

Cara waited, her throat tightening. "What?"

"Vanessa's taking riding lessons on Lucas!" Sophie blurted.

Cara couldn't believe she was hearing right. "No!" she cried. "He's terrified of her."

"He doesn't like it at all," Sophie admitted. "But thank goodness Ms. P.'s in charge. She watches both of them every second."

Cara smiled grimly. She could imagine Ms. P.'s reaction to Vanessa riding Lucas.

"What's Vanessa like with him?" she asked nervously.

"She yells a lot, trying to cover up how scared she really is," Sophie replied.

Cara forced herself to ask the question she didn't want to know the answer to. "Does she hurt him?"

"No," Sophie answered honestly. She smiled gently at Cara's worried face. "He doesn't like her, but he's gentleman enough to put up with her bad manners."

Cara shook her head, bewildered. "I wonder what she's scheming up now?"

169

"Maybe she's just trying to get back into Mom's good graces."

Cara visited Lucas in secret the next day. He was hot and strained, even more out of condition than a week before. She felt useless, utterly hopeless—what was upsetting him so much? In desperation she phoned Ms. P.

"It's not Vanessa," she assured Cara. "He doesn't like her, but she doesn't hurt him. I make quite sure of that!" But Cara continued to worry, all through the week at school.

"I feel weird," she told Tansy as they were eating lunch.

"How, weird?"

"As if I'm waiting for something terrible to happen," Cara explained.

"Are you psychic or something?" Tansy teased, but Cara was deadly serious.

"No, it's nothing like that. I just know Lucas—I understand him," she said. "What he needs right now is loving and looking after, not rough treatment. He's scared stiff of Vanessa."

"But he does belong to her," Tansy pointed out. "And there's not much you or anybody can do about that!"

"Okay, okay," Cara said wearily. "But nothing can stop me from worrying about him."

Unfortunately because nothing could stop Cara from worrying about Lucas, nothing could keep her away from him on Saturday morning, when she knew Vanessa had a lesson. She had to be there.

On Saturday Cara took the bus and hid in the woods. If she stood on tiptoe, she could see Sophie tacking Lucas up. She ducked under cover when she saw Ms. P. and Vanessa head toward the warm-up ring. Peering through the bushes, she could just make out what was going on. She saw Sophie begin her warm-up exercises. Sophie practiced her posting trot, watched by Ms. P. and Vanessa, who paced irritably around the ring. Afraid of being seen, Cara slipped under the bushes and listened hard. The birds whistled, bees droned, and a slight breeze stirred in the treetops. Everything seemed so peaceful.

Let's hope it stays that way, Cara thought.

Suddenly she heard Vanessa snap impatiently, "Come on, Sophie. Let me have a turn. I'm bored stiff watching you!"

Sophie reluctantly dismounted, and Vanessa snatched the reins from her. Cara saw Lucas back off nervously, and her heart froze. Ms. P. moved toward Vanessa, but Vanessa ignored her and threw herself heavily into the saddle, giving Lucas an ungracious kick in the ribs. Lucas nervously threw back his head, and Vanessa sawed at his mouth with the reins.

"Stop her, Ms. P.," Cara murmured.

It was obvious that Ms. P. was trying to tell Vanessa something, but Vanessa wouldn't listen to her. She kept kicking Lucas in the ribs and yanking at his mouth with the reins. From the woods Cara could see Lucas was winding up like a spring. In her anxiety she forgot about hiding herself and ran toward them, crying, "No! *No!*"

171

Vanessa spotted Cara, and her face darkened with fury. Grabbing Ms. P.'s whip, she lashed at Lucas's hindquarters. He shot forward wildly, out of control. Vanessa screamed and dropped the reins as he headed for the ring fence.

"Sit forward!" Cara shouted, even though she knew it was pointless.

Lucas zoomed over the fence with his unwieldy rider. Clinging to Lucas's neck, Vanessa continued to scream as he broke into a full gallop and headed down the drive, straight toward the main road. Everybody was running after them, but not fast enough.

"Get in my car!" yelled Ms. P. Sophie and Cara dashed to the station wagon and jumped in.

"Hold on tight," Ms. P. said, and drove full speed down the drive. They rounded a bend just in time to see Lucas jump a hedge, this time unseating Vanessa. She flipped over his head and fell hard on her shoulders. Gradually Lucas began to slow down, and finally stopped.

"Let me get him," Cara begged.

Ms. P. stopped the car by Vanessa, who lay white and unconscious in the mud. Cara gently approached Lucas. He was shuddering all over, cut and bleeding from bumping into bushes during their wild ride, eyes rolling. He hardly seemed to recognize her and backed away, his nostrils dilated with fear.

"Lucas, it's me," she whispered.

Hearing her voice seemed to calm him. His

breathing slowly eased, and his head stopped jerking. She gathered up his tangled reins and with infinite tenderness ran her hands along his neck.

"Shh, shh, it's all right," she murmured. She talked to him and stroked him until he seemed completely calmed down, then quietly walked him back to the stable. There she untacked him and washed his wounds. He seemed exhausted and afraid, and nuzzled her for reassurance.

"I'll look after you, just for a while," she promised.

She had never felt so useless. Lucas, the love of her life, was permanently at risk, and all she ever seemed to do was stand by and watch it happen. If she was lucky, she was allowed to pick up the pieces—wash his wounds, groom him down, calm him—and for what? The next attack! Surely somebody could stop this cruelty!

As if in answer to her thoughts, Ms. P. walked in. "How is he?" she asked.

"Terrified," Cara answered.

Ms. P. sighed and leaned against the stall door. "This *has* to stop," she said.

"Yes, but when?" Cara asked.

Ms. P. sighed heavily. "Pretty soon, I think. Vanessa's broken her arm."

"Too bad it wasn't her neck," Cara said coldly.

"She's at the hospital. She'll be there overnight," added Ms. P. "Now tell me, Cara, why were you hiding in the woods?"

"I just knew something was going to happen," Cara answered truthfully.

"Standing up and shouting didn't help much," Ms. P. pointed out.

"I know, and I'm sorry," Cara said. "But Vanessa would have made trouble anyway—whether I jumped out of the woods or not."

"Yes, you're right," Ms. P. agreed. "She was headed for a bruising from the minute she showed up today. She wouldn't listen to a word I said."

"How's Mrs. Deneuve?" Cara asked.

"Frightened, I think," said Ms. P. "The whole situation has gotten badly out of control. Her idea of living in rural bliss has backfired disastrously. None of the county set that she's so eager to befriend will have anything to do with her since the finals. They were all, quite rightly, appalled by Vanessa's outrageous behavior there."

Cara nodded. Who wouldn't have been?

"I feel quite sorry for her," continued Ms. P. "She has tried hard, and for all her silly ways she never intended to hurt anybody. But . . ." Her eyes followed the lines of Lucas's bleeding cuts. "Everybody's come out of it badly, especially this poor boy."

Cara's eyes filled with tears. "I don't want to lose him," she sobbed. "But I wish Mrs. Deneuve would sell him. At least he'd be away from here, out of danger."

"I'm sure that's what will happen," said Ms. P. "Nobody in their right mind would want this to go on." She sighed heavily. "You could say Vanessa's won." Throwing her arm around Cara's shaking shoulders, she said, "Come on, time to take you home."

174

With a bowed head Cara followed Ms. P. to her battered old car. Her premonitions of danger had been bad enough, but reality would be worse—a future forever without Lucas.

15

EVENTS MOVED QUICKLY AFTER VANESSA CAME OUT OF THE hospital. Predictably she made the most of everything, even getting her photograph in the local paper with an article portraying her as the innocent victim of a nasty riding accident.

"She really will stop at nothing," said Ms. P. in disgust.

Cara waited tensely, sensing more was to follow. She was right. It was Sophie who finally broke the news. She phoned Cara on Saturday, a week after the accident, and told her that Mrs. Deneuve was selling Lucas.

Cara felt her blood turn to ice, but she reminded herself that Lucas's situation had to change, for his sake. "He'll be better off," she managed to say. "At least he won't be anywhere near Vanessa."

Sophie burst into tears. "I know, I know," she got out. "I've been telling myself that too. But . . ." She struggled for breath. "I'll miss him so much."

Cara swallowed, unable to speak. Tears flowed silently down her face and trickled over the telephone. "We'll *all* miss him," she finally managed.

She felt sorry for Sophie. In Sophie's family, the battle always seemed to be between Mrs. Deneuve and Vanessa. Sophie's needs came second, or not at all. Nobody had even considered *her* achievements. She'd been hauled into the country, sent to a school she'd never liked, bought a horse she was terrified of—and commanded to ride!

"Look, you've done really well since you've been here," Cara said. "You learned not to be afraid of horses and to ride. And best of all, you learned to love Lucas."

Sophie laughed with delight. "Come on, Cara, loving Lucas was the easy part."

"And now, just when you've got everything going for you, it's being taken away!" Cara cried. "That's not fair, Sophie—it's just not fair."

Sophie shrugged. "I'm used to it," she murmured.

"Then stop getting used to it!" Cara said. "Have you asked your mom if you can keep Lucas?"

"Not a chance!" Sophie exclaimed. "He's better off away from this place."

Cara couldn't really argue with that.

"Mom thinks the sooner Lucas is gone, the better," Sophie said.

Cara felt the color drain from her face.

"But hold on," Sophie quickly added. "Here's the good news—he's going to Ms. P.'s riding school until he's sold."

"Really?" Cara cried, her heart suddenly lifting. "I'll be able to see him *every day*!"

"That's right," Sophie said. "You've got at least a little longer together."

Cara virtually lived at Hunters' Riding School for the next two weeks. Nobody stopped her, troubled her, or spoiled her precious time with Lucas. Away from Vanessa and reunited with Cara, Lucas flourished. His coat came back, gleaming gold. His eyes were bright and lively, he gained weight quickly—even his mane seemed longer!

As long as Cara didn't think about the future she was fine. *I'll take each day as it comes*, she said to herself every morning when she woke up, *and be grateful for what I've got*. But when the advertisement went into the newspapers and magazines and people began calling with inquiries, reality hit her like a brick.

How long have I got with him? she wondered every night. *Hours or days?*

She was startled by his selling price. It was low—still far too expensive for her, but low.

"Mrs. Deneuve wants a quick sale," Ms. P. explained.

It was a relief for everyone when Sophie said that Vanessa had gone off to Washington for the summer. *At least*, Cara thought, *she won't be able to badmouth Lucas during the sale*.

Sophie said Mrs. Deneuve was rethinking her own position. She really wasn't enjoying country life as much as she thought she would. She hadn't made many friends, wasn't invited to the social events she'd set her hopes on, and hadn't even learned to ride or succeeded in getting her daughters to be competent riders. The experiment hadn't worked. She was, however, thinking of renting a cottage in Virginia for vacations. As usual, Sophie had gotten the rotten end of the deal.

"You can always come and stay with me," Cara assured her.

"And me," added Ms. P. "I need a good stable hand during vacations."

Sophie stared at her, astonished. "Me!" she gasped. "Work here and help you?"

Ms. P. nodded. "Of course," she said. "I taught you—you must be good!"

Cara found that she was strangely happy. Each extra minute with Lucas was a gift. When he was grazing in the paddock, the sun glinting on his summer coat, now glowing with health, she was happy just to stand by the fence and watch him. She followed the dip of his graceful head as he bent to nibble the grass, the exquisite shape of his soft nose, the set of his hindquarters, the golden swish of his tail. She loved the way his ears pricked at the sound of her footsteps, and the heart-melting softness of his dark eyes as he raised his head to gaze at her. It was that look of love that had pierced her heart over a year ago and still had the same effect on her now. She etched every detail of him in her memory, trying to make a perfect picture she would carry in her mind forever.

Lucas too seemed to sense that their time was precious. He was devoted to Cara, following her across the paddock and around the stable yard as if he were her puppy. As he trotted behind her he'd nudge her in the back with his nose or huff into her hair, blowing it all over her face. She'd turn around and pretend to glare at him.

"You bad boy!" she would scold, but his soft, sweet expression made her dissolve. Instead of being firm, she'd throw her arms around his neck and kiss his nose.

Although Cara had prepared herself, nothing could have stopped her heart from freezing up when Ms. P. said, "Lucas has been sold."

Cara felt her knees buckle, and her head started to spin. She quickly leaned against the stable wall before she fell over.

"When?" she gasped.

"He'll be picked up this weekend," Ms. P. said. "Believe me, he's going to a good home—the best."

Cara nodded. "Good, that's good," she repeated like a parrot.

The next two days were agony for Cara. She couldn't bear to be away from Lucas for a minute. She'd counted the days they had left; now she was counting the hours. She never thought to ask who had bought him or where he was going. Their life together was over. She didn't want to make a scene about it or make Lucas unhappy, though—he'd had enough of that at the Deneuves' to last him the rest of his life.

On Saturday Cara was at Ms. P.'s school just after dawn. She picked up Lucas's halter from the stable and went into the paddock to get him. Standing in a drift of early morning mist, knee deep in tall grass and buttercups, Lucas looked like a dream of the perfect horse. Seeing her he trotted over, ears pricked, eyes curious and bright.

"Oh, Lucas!" she cried. "If only you weren't so beautiful!"

She groomed him and tacked him up in the stable, and then they went out for their last ride. He started off eagerly, but as they cantered down the paths he slowed his pace and walked back to the stable rather subdued.

Cara talked to him as she untacked him. "You're going to a new home," she said. "A good home, where you'll be better looked after, I promise you."

Lucas listened, his eyes dark and serious, his head slightly to one side. Suddenly he stomped his hoof on the stable floor and nudged her impatiently. He seemed to sense something important was going to happen. Wrapping her arms around his neck, she whispered, "You're going away, darling horse. We won't see each other again."

Lucas nudged her, and she looked into his eyes. They stared at each other, and Cara knew that he somehow understood. Bending her head to touch his, she stood with him quietly, silently saying a last good-bye.

Suddenly wheels scrunched on gravel. The horse van had arrived to take him away.

Mrs. Deneuve had turned up to complete the business. A kind-looking middle-aged man, who Cara was sure she'd seen at the finals, got out of the van. He shook Mrs. Deneuve's hand and they went into Ms. P.'s office, leaving Cara to load Lucas. For the first time ever Lucas stopped on the ramp. He stood and looked around the stable yard, then whinnied shrilly to the other horses.

Inside the van, Cara thought her heart would break with grief. As she tied Lucas up and loaded his tack, tears flowed unchecked down her face. When everything was done, she laid her head against his neck.

"I'll always, *always* love you," she sobbed. She had to be led out of the van by Ms. P., who quickly slammed the gate shut.

The middle-aged man came out of the office, shook Mrs. Deneuve's hand, and climbed into the driver's seat. When the engine started, Lucas stamped hard, and as they drove out of the gate a loud whinny burst out of the van. As the sound of his good-bye tore through her heart Cara knew that something inside her had died forever.

Beyond tears, she returned to his stall, where the air was still warm with his smell. Clutching his lead rope like a lifeline, Cara stared wildly around her. Suddenly she saw Sophie's face framed in the doorway.

"Do you want to go for a walk?" she said.

Cara shook her head.

"Please come," Sophie insisted. "You need to get away from here."

Cara ignored her. She wanted to stay in Lucas's stall and be alone with her pain.

"Please?" Sophie begged.

Cara suddenly realized Sophie might be suffering too. After all, Lucas had belonged to her.

She nodded. "Okay."

They walked in silence out of the yard and across the open fields. Neither of them spoke. It was good to walk, to feel the sun on her face and hear the birdsong. They walked for about half a mile, then Sophie stopped.

"Do you want to go back?" Cara asked.

Sophie shook her head and smiled mysteriously. "No," she said. "I want to show you something."

Cara was in no mood for games. "Not now," she snapped, and headed back the way they'd come. Sophie ran after her.

"It won't take a minute!" she cried, grabbing Cara by the arm. "Look—" She pointed to a distant field.

Cara followed the line of her trembling finger. All she could see was a horse in a field.

"What?" she asked irritably.

"*Look!*" Sophie yelled.

Again Cara stared . . . and suddenly her eyes detected a glint of gold. Leaving Sophie, she ran across the fields and stopped dead in her tracks. Standing there, looking as baffled as she felt, was Lucas! Sophie caught up with her, gasping for breath.

Cara turned on her. "Don't do this to me!" she screamed. "Don't keep making me say good-bye to him!"

183

Sophie took her arm and shook it. "Cara, listen to me," she said. "It's not good-bye—" She stopped and gulped. "He's *yours!*"

Cara stared at her, her eyes wide with disbelief. "Mine? *No!* He's just been sold!"

"That's right—we bought him for you." Sophie pointed down the path to the parked horse van. Beside it stood Mr. and Mrs. Zol and Ms. P.

"You . . . *did?*" Cara spluttered. Breaking into a run, she tore across the field to her parents.

"Mom! Dad!" she cried, throwing herself into their open arms. "Tell me what's going on!"

"It'll take a while, honey," said her dad, grinning. "It's a long story." He patted the grass beside him. "Come on, sit down and I'll tell you."

Cara sat beside him, her eyes burning into Lucas.

"As you know, your mom and I never had the money to buy you a horse of your own."

Cara nodded. She knew *that* better than anybody.

"But when Lucas came up for sale at such a low price, Ms. P. suggested we buy him for you."

Cara stared at Ms. P. Tears filled her eyes.

"Well, your mom and I had a little money saved, Ms. P. made a contribution and so did Joseph, and Mike gave us most of the contents of his piggybank." He smiled. "Sophie too." He nodded toward Sophie, who was shyly hanging back. "And then, would you believe it, just when we thought we couldn't get quite enough money together, a check turned up for you. Your winnings from the finals!" Her dad smiled triumphantly. "That clinched the deal." Cara shook her head, unable to speak. Her father seemed pretty choked up too. "So that was it—we were in business," he finished. He turned to Ms. P. "You take over."

"We knew that Mrs. Deneuve would never sell Lucas to us," said Ms. P. "She wanted him out of the county, as far away from Vanessa as possible." She paused and smiled. "I can see her point, really. So we roped in a very good friend of mine—"

"The man who picked up Lucas!" Cara interrupted, suddenly remembering who the middle-aged man was. "Your friend from the finals."

Ms. P. nodded and smiled broadly.

"I knew I'd seen him before," said Cara.

"We gave him the money and he bought Lucas for us," explained Ms. P. "Lucky for us, the price was low."

Cara shook her head. "This is incredible!" she murmured.

"I'm sorry we put you through so much," Sophie whispered, hugging her. "I nearly told you about a hundred times. You were so unhappy."

"You've suffered enough," Ms. P. said. "None of us wanted you to suffer anymore."

Cara turned to her parents and her friends, feeling a mixture of love, gratitude, and complete disbelief.

"But I'm happy *now*!" she cried. "Thank you, thank you, thank you," she said, hugging each of them in turn. "I'll remember this my whole life!"

A shrill whinny caught her complete attention. With a blissful smile, she turned to see Lucas. "Will you excuse me, please?" she asked them.

She set off toward her horse, her face radiant. "Lucas!" she called.

Whinnying with joy, he trotted toward her, not for one treat or cuddle, but for the start of their life together. She took in every detail of him, from his exquisite head down his neck to his muscular shoulders, and along his hindquarters to the golden shower of his tail.

"You're mine," she whispered. "Mine—and I'll never, *ever* let you go again!"

ABOUT DIANE REDMOND

I live in Cambridge, England, with my three children, three labradors, and two horses. We live in the city, which is very old and beautiful, and we have to travel five miles to get to our stable. It's worth the trouble though. The first thing we see every time we drive up is Lucas peering over the gate, waiting for us, and Tara peering over Lucas, desperate for a sweet! Lucas is an Irish draft horse like the one in this story, and Tara is an extremely fat twenty-year-old Shetland pony. They make a very comical pair. When Tara gets fed up with Lucas bossing and pushing her about, she turns back on him and kicks him in the teeth!

I've written lots of books, for children of all ages, including a novel for teenage girls and boys about football, which will be serialized to coincide with the World Cup 1994. I've written television and radio scripts, presented my own television series, and written several plays for the London theater, the Edinburgh Festival, and the Cambridge Youth Theatre.

▉ HarperPaperbacks *By Mail*

Read all the T H O R O U G H B R E D books
by Joanna Campbell

#1 A Horse Called Wonder   #5 Ashleigh's Dream
#2 Wonder's Promise   #6 Wonder's Yearling
#3 Wonder's First Race   #7 Samantha's Pride
#4 Wonder's Victory   #8 Sierra's Steeplechase

And don't miss these other great horse books:

The Forgotten Filly by Karle Dickerson

When Joelle's mare, Dance Away, dies, Joelle swears that no horse will ever take her place—especially not Dance Away's filly. Then something amazing happens to change her mind. . . .

Christmas Colt by Mallory Stevens

Chrissie can't wait to get rid of her Christmas present—a scraggly colt. But as the annual auction approaches, "Klutz" develops into a beautiful yearling. Will Chrissie lose the horse she has grown to love?

And look for the complete *Across the Wild River* adventure trilogy:

#1 Across the Wild River   **#2 Along the Dangerous Trail**

#3 Over the Rugged Mountain

MAIL TO: Harper Collins Publishers
P.O.Box 588, Dunmore, PA 18512-0588

TELEPHONE: 1-800-331-3716 (Visa and Mastercard holders!)
YES, please send me the following titles:

❏ A Horse Called Wonder (0-06-106120-4) $3.50
❏ Wonder's Promise (0-06-106085-2) $3.50
❏ Wonder's First Race (0-06-106082-8) $3.50
❏ Wonder's Victory (0-06-106083-6) $3.50
❏ Ashleigh's Dream (0-06-106737-7)...$3.50
❏ Wonder's Yearling (0-06-106747-4) $3.50
❏ Samantha's Pride (0-06-106163-8)...$3.50

❏ Forgotten Filly (0-06-106732-6)..$3.50
❏ Christmas Colt (0-06-106721-0)..$3.50

❏ Across the Wild River (0-06-106159-X) $3.50
❏ Along the Dangerous Trail (0-06-106152-2) $3.50

SUBTOTAL ....$_____
POSTAGE AND HANDLING* ....$ 2.00
SALES TAX (Add applicable state sales tax) ....$_____

TOTAL: ....$_____
(Remit in U.S. funds. Do not send cash.)

NAME_____
ADDRESS_____
CITY_____
STATE_____ ZIP _____

Allow up to six weeks for delivery. Prices subject to change. Valid only in U.S. and Canada.

*Free postage/handling if you buy four or more!